Avoiding Mr. Right

A Walk on the Wild Side Novel

C.J. Ellisson

Red Hot Publishing
P.O. BOX 651193, STERLING VA, 20165-1193

First ebook Edition June 2013
First Print Edition Dec 2013

Edited by Tina Winograd
Cover Design by Kim Killion, HotDamnDesigns.com

eBook ISBN 9781938601156
Print ISBN 9781938601187

PUBLISHER'S NOTE
This is a work of fiction. Names, characters, places, and incidents are either the products of the author's imagination or are used fictitiously, and any resemblance to actual persons, living or dead, business establishments, events, or locales is entirely coincidental.

This book is dedicated to Marianne Morea and T. Lynne Tolles. Your work is more than worthy—and soon the world will know it. Never give up!

Chapter One

Carla

"*Casual Sex*," I say, twisting the phrase so it sounds like a bad thing. "There. I said it." I look across the table and meet my best friend's dark, knowing gaze. "Happy now?" Unable to hold her penetrating stare any longer, I reach for my tepid chai latte, grateful it's tasty even when cold.

"I know you think I'm being a shrewish bitch, Carla. But it's for your own good." Heather picks up her favorite vanilla cappuccino and takes a drink.

"And why is that, exactly?" Regret gnaws at my stomach. Why did I let myself get dragged into this conversation during my lunch hour? "Sure, you found your great 'one-and-only' guy, but I don't think that's going to happen with me."

Heather ignores me and taps her finger on the small sheet of paper on the table between us. "Next one."

Geez, this feels like a one-woman intervention, and despite the jokes I could make over that realization, I'm really *not* enjoying it. The pleading on her compassionate face has me glancing at the slip of paper once more. "*Friends with Benefits*. Oh, come on, that too? I kind of like that one. Makes it much easier to stay friends when the guy winds up being dumb, but not bad in bed."

Heather's mouth sets in a firm line and I plow ahead to the last item on her unhelpful "list" of what she sees as my love life faults. "*Avoidance of Intimacy*. Seriously? You think I do all this crap?" A knot of anxiety sits in my throat. "I'm not a fun-loving chick all the time, you know. I have been searching for the right guy." The right guy who's perfect in the sack and magically disappears before dawn. "Just haven't found him yet."

"Really?" she counters, showing a touch of backbone my once-shy friend didn't have a month ago. "And none of them were *worthy* of your time after you slept with them, huh?"

A grimace twists my face and I try to smooth my features. "It's not like that—I swear." Secretly I fear it's *exactly* like that. And what the hell does that say about me? That I'm a slut? I'm not. I like sex but I don't sleep with just anyone like her darned unasked for list of faults implies. "They weren't good matches for me."

"Uh-huh. Sure."

"Why are we discussing this...," I gesture to the paper between us, "*list* of yours? I'm a careful woman. I always make sure they use a condom. My instincts are good. I've never been in a situation I couldn't handle. What happened to make you think I needed—no *wanted*—your input in my love life?"

Heather's strength deflates and I feel like I've kicked a puppy. "It's because I care about you, Carla, and want to see you happy. You keep up with this casual approach to relationships and you're going to be alone for the rest of your life."

A snort erupts from me. "Like that's a bad thing? I'm not afraid of being alone. In fact, I'm quite all right with it." I resist the urge, just barely, to throw her words from a few weeks ago in her face. *She* was the one afraid of winding up alone and eating microwave meals-for-one her whole life. Not me. Never me.

My goal has always been to find an exciting, independent man—one who's a great lover *and* wants nothing emotional from me in return. I gaze out the window of our favorite coffee shop, staring at the pelting rain washing the city streets. Maybe my relaxed attitude would be better suited in Europe. Seems like the Puritanical ideals of America are still going strong, no matter how much women struggle with equality. If I were a guy no one would bat an eye at my desire for a lover with no emotional attachments weighing us down.

An exciting man who's good in bed. That's not too much to ask is it? We're in "the city that never sleeps" for crying out loud. There's got to be a few guys who learned *something* in the sack since college, right? Maybe I can find one who isn't emotionally scarred from a long-term relationship *and* where the woman taught him a thing or two. That would be hitting the relationship lottery in my book.

Don't forget good looking, great body, successful career, a big dick...

Yeah, a girl can dream, right?

Aware I need to get back to work, I glance at my watch then gather the remains of my meal. We say our goodbyes and I race into the rain, pulling up the hood on my stylish raincoat for the three-block trek to the office.

Heather likes to forget—I'm not like her. I've always known what I want in my life *and* in my bed. She and Tony met at the exact time she was ready to blossom. My sexuality bloomed a long time ago and I quickly became disappointed with the unknowledgeable lovers I invited into my bed. Hell, when the first few trysts were a let down, why go back for more?

It's pretty sad, really. They all appeared to be so promising during our initial dates.

Despite Heather's list making me sound like a "good-time girl," a phrase I hear a lot from my mom, I actually practice a lot of decorum when choosing a lover. They all have ambitious careers, their own apartments, aren't married, and know how to treat a lady with manners. I don't have a set laundry list of physical attributes the guy has to have, but I do want a man who cares enough about his health and appearance to not be slovenly or obese.

Unlike Heather, I never sit on the sidelines waiting for life to come to me—I actively seek adventure and always will. Who says a woman needs a man to be happy? I'm happy as I am on my own. And I intend to keep it that way—not hung up on a guy like my mom was with my dad. When he left us, she was devastated and it changed her outlook on life forever.

Avoiding large puddles and dangerous sidewalk grating, I wish I would've changed out of my heels before dashing off to meet Heather. A short woman like me learns the benefit of being on equal eye level in the advertising world. Doesn't hurt that I look great in them, too.

The awning to my building appears and I gratefully step under it and push back my hood. I unzip the coat and flap the sides, knocking off moisture before entering.

"Hey, Carla," a masculine voice calls from the doorway.

I look up to see one of the company accountants holding the door for me. "Thanks, Andrew." I step through, avoiding eye contact with him.

He's tried to make casual conversation with me for months, and I'm always polite but careful not to lead him on. I mean really, he's an *accountant*. Could a job be more unexciting? Just stick him in an IT position and buy him a ticket to the next Trekkie convention in town.

One thing I've learned while shopping for an exciting man—I won't find one in a humdrum job like his. I'm not saying Andrew is boring, he seems nice enough. But his job sure as hell is unexciting, which decreases his chances of being a stimulating guy by eighty percent.

While we walk across the lobby to the elevators, I sense him fidgeting beside me, perhaps too nervous to talk. I smother a smile at his awkwardness. Honestly, he's not bad looking—no beer gut and he dresses okay. Maybe

I should hook him up with Katrina from yoga class. She's been on the prowl for a decent man.

He clears his throat as we step into the elevator. "Do you have time later to talk about the Stringer account?"

My ears perk at the mention of my largest client. "Of course. Is something wrong?"

The doors whisk closed and we ascend to our floor. "No, nothing's wrong. I was looking over the latest numbers and think I've found a way to free up some advertising money in their budget that isn't working where it is now. Might help you up-sell them to a larger ad space in the areas that are working."

"Sounds good." I smile, the first genuine one to grace my face since I met Heather for lunch. "Your cubicle or mine?"

His blue eyes crinkle at the corners as he returns my smile. "Come to mine, I'll show you the spreadsheets."

Hours later I hang up the phone with Jennifer Stringer, the owner of the largest independently owned fabric distributor in the legendary New York garment district. She was thrilled with Andrew's findings and eager to pour fifty thousand more into the current advertising campaign. We helped to increase her business twenty percent in the last three months. Satisfaction for a job well done warms me, filling me with a sense of completeness like no encounter with a man ever has.

A sigh escapes as I relax into my chair. Damn, talk about a long week. It's Friday and after five. I stifle the urge to chant *TGIF* and log off my computer, eager to shake the stresses of the week from my shoulders.

IMs flew around the office ten minutes ago and people are gearing up to meet at the bar down the block for drinks. I freshen my lipstick, straighten my desk, and grab my bag. Andrew stands the same moment I do and our eyes meet across the cubical walls. "Are you going tonight?" I ask him.

Interest lights his eyes. "Yup."

He runs a hand through his short brown hair, the gesture making him appear more confident. Too bad he's boring, he's almost handsome. "Great, I owe you a drink for that tidbit you shared after lunch."

A small smile turns up his mouth as he walks down the opposite aisle toward the door. "Just one? Could have sworn my 'tidbit' helped you make your monthly quota a week early."

I laugh at his ballsiness. "Maybe I'll buy you two. But don't get your hopes up."

A spark ignites in his blue depths as his gaze travels up and down my length. An awareness tingles through me and I can't deny, he looks *different*, somehow. He's only a few inches taller than I am in heels, which makes him a couple of inches shy of six-foot. His shirtsleeves are rolled up to reveal corded forearms with a light dusting of hair. With warm heat banked in his gaze, his average looks jump a thousand points.

I brush off the sudden interest spiking in my gut. I can't let an office romance begin to brew. I told Heather I wasn't doing any of the things she accused me of. No matter how much I might wish otherwise, I highly doubt a *co-worker with benefits* is much different than the *friends with benefits* on her sheet.

As a large boisterous group of our co-workers join us in the elevator, I resolve to steer clear of any temptation offered by Andrew at the bar. No way in the world could he be a good match for me.

Chapter Two

Andrew

Bodies press against Carla, shoving her closer to the bar as she tries to leave the stool. I reach out an arm to protect her from the worst of the crush. “Carla, let me see you home. You shouldn’t make your way alone.”

Her buzzed smile and feeling-no-pain expression is a sure sign we should have had dinner when the bartender offered menus an hour ago.

“No worries, Andy. I’m good.” She stumbles and lands face first against the broad chest of a nearby guy. The grin on his face shows he’s not angry at her slip.

“My...you’re big,” she says while pushing blond bangs out of her face. “Want to help me get a cab?”

Anger boils close to the surface at the mere thought of the curvy blonde going home with this meathead. I will not stand here and let her make a poor choice when she's been drinking. The large man opens his mouth to respond, then catches sight of what I hope is a nasty look on my face. His smile dims as he looks back to Carla. "Maybe next time, sweetheart."

I nod my thanks while trying to steer my more than tipsy co-worker out of our company's favorite after-work bar.

"But, Andy," she whines, "he looked hot. Lemme get his number."

I take a firm hold on her arm and gently maneuver her toward the door. "You'll thank me later."

The cool late spring air smacks us, jolting me with a much-needed surge of energy. Hopefully, it will have the same affect on Carla. "But, he looks like a *real man*," she says, with a pointed look my way.

I ignore the brush of annoyance I feel at her implication I'm not a real man. Where the hell is her aggravation coming from? "Yeah, and I'm sure he'll call you in the morning, too."

"That's not fair, Andy. The guy I picked up two months ago called me."

I hail a taxi and pour us inside.

"But he turned out to be dumb." She snorts at a memory while I tell the cabbie her address. In the ensuing silence she whispers, "Couldn't even find my clit."

I resist shaking her for her stupid actions. I know firsthand she has a solid mind and a sharp wit. It's the alcohol getting to her, and it's getting to me, too. The mere mention of sex has parts of me growing in my suit pants. She settles snug against my side, hugging my arm. "Whoa, Andy. You have some serious muscles here. Have you been working out?"

Her grasping fingers massage my bicep through my jacket. "I've always worked out." I pry away her grip then she squeals and aims to tickle me. Bad move. Her quick hands graze my expanding arousal and she freezes.

"Andy! Do you want me?" A wisp of longing sounds in her voice.

I suppress the sigh aching to burst forth. I've wanted Carla from the moment we teamed up on the Stringer account six months ago, but needed to wait for the right time to approach her. And partially drunk is not the right time. "Carla, let's just get you home. We've both been drinking and I don't want to do anything we may regret later."

She nips playfully at my ear. “How could I possibly regret fooling around with you? We could be *friends with benefits*. Wouldn’t that be cool?”

“While the idea sounds excellent, I’m not so sure it ever works.”

“Oh, come on. You’re starting to sound like my friend, Heather. I like sex... it’s fun. It never hurt anyone.” Her previously frozen hand strokes my erection through the fabric.

Dear God, are we almost to her building? I need to get her off me and out of this cab before I come in my pants.

“We could make it work, Andy. Despite what Heather says.” She pulls her hand from my erection and turns my face to hers for a kiss, moisture gleaming in her eyes. “We could try.”

Excitement courses through me. Her breath smells sweetly of white wine and I want nothing more than to crush my mouth to hers and devour her whole. Energy seems to leap from my lips to hers as I lean in, succumbing to the raging desire to possess her.

The taxi lurches to a stop, jerking us toward the front of the cab, breaking the spell a moment before our lips touch. The fog of lust clears from my mind and I want to ask about Heather and what she may have said to upset Carla, but instead I fish out the cash to pay the driver.

I impulsively decide to walk her to her door. Maybe we could make this work. I admit I want more from her and this night of fun might be a good place to start.

She grabs my hand and playfully drags me past her doorman. I nod at the man, feeling a shit-eating grin spread across my features. "Come on, Andy," she loudly whispers, her voice carrying easily across the lobby, "let's have dinner at my place."

The walk through the lobby doesn't cool our previous heat and the moment the elevator doors whisk shut, Carla is on me like a tick on a dog. Her full mouth crushes mine and manicured nails rake through my hair. Instantly, my erection surges, pressing against my zipper, straining to get closer to this sexy woman.

I pull back from the intense kiss and mutter, "What floor?"

"Nineteen." She gasps and locks her mouth to mine again. I press the button and the car ascends.

"God, Andy, I'm so freakin' hot right now." She thrusts her hips to mine, grinding against my hardness. "Want to do it here in the elevator?"

I wrap my hands around her hips and leverage her slightly away from the front of my pants. "As good as that sounds, I don't think we should."

"Pfff... you're no fun, Andy." She reaches for my zipper and has my cock in her hot little hand before I can grab her wrist. "Ohh... but this looks like it could lead to a lot of fun."

The elevator pings and I jerk in surprise. The doors slide open ten floors shy of her level. Panic surges and I wrap my arms around my curvy, drunken co–worker, pinning her to me—not wanting the older man in workout gear who just stepped into the car to see me hanging out of my pants.

He glances at us, hits the button next to the word "Gym", then stands on the far side.

Carla giggles, but thankfully shoves my cock into my pants and then yanks up the zipper. The rasp of metal on metal brings a sharp look from the man, but his head whips around to face straight ahead.

We finally arrive at Carla's floor and rush off the elevator. Adrenaline floods my body and I swear, if she asks, I'm going to follow her in and screw this horny woman senseless.

"Andy?" Carla asks, a hopeful note in her tone. "Want to come in?"

Tension I didn't know I was holding eases out of me. I move behind her while she jiggles her key into the lock and wrap myself around her slight frame. Planting kisses along her neck, I give the only answer my fired up body will allow. "I'd love to."

When the door closes behind us, it's a mad dash to see who can get their clothes off faster. Glimpses of black underwear and toned limbs whir through my alcohol fogged brain.

Carla giggles while stumbling to her bedroom. She switches on the bedside light and tosses me what she must think is a sexy smile, but looks more like a slight sneer. "Come and get me, Mr. Super Accountant."

I hesitate in the doorway. Parts of me rage to barrel forward and take her up on her offer before she changes her mind, but my big head gets the best of me. "Are you sure, Carla? You want to take this step?"

She reaches between her legs and starts to touch herself. "If you aren't interested, I'll handle things on my own." I approach the bed, determination firming my mouth. "Good boy, I knew you'd come around."

Climbing across the mattress, I crawl on hands and knees to cover her lithe form. Her hips thrust up to meet mine while grasping hands pull me down. "Now, Andy. I want you *now*."

"Whoa, slow down. We need protection."

"You're right." Giggling again, she twists to the side, then reaches into the nightstand drawer to pull out a small foil square. Carla tears it with her teeth, her face scrunching up. "Ewww... spermicide tastes like crap."

Taking the torn package from her, I remove the latex and sheath myself as fast as possible.

"Get it in, get it in, get it in..." she chants. I position myself at her entrance, wishing we'd slowed down a little bit. Her hips push forward as she impales herself on my length. "Oh..." she moans as I finish the first stroke in, burying deep inside, "that's right."

The orders start flying before I have a chance to slow her down: "Faster!" "Harder!" "Slam it in me!"

Thrusting my hips in a frenzy, I try to fulfill each request the second it's uttered. The hot, inner muscles of her body encircle my length, and the speed combines with my buzz to push me toward the finish before I'd like.

"I'm close, Carla. I need to slow down."

"No! More! Do me harder!"

Nails rake along my spine and hot hands grab my ass, pulling me closer despite my desire to wait. Her feet splay on the bed, pushing up her hips to pump me when I hold back.

The sensations overwhelm my control and my orgasm steams past the gates. A loud moan spills from my mouth. I try to keep up the pace a little longer, hoping to bring her as well. "Are you close?"

But Carla's quiet. A glance reveals her eyelids are drifting closed, and I can feel her hips have stopped moving. "Carla?"

"Umm?"

"Did you come?"

"Are we done?" She yawns. "Gosh, I'm sleepy."

I roll to the side, snatching some tissues to clean up. This may have been a very bad idea. She doesn't seem to be aware I came. "Carla?" I say, fitting my body snug against her back. "Would you like to feel my mouth? Or my hand?"

"Nah, 's all good," she slurs while turning onto her side to pillow an arm under her cheek.

Her breathing deepens and I'm left wondering what the hell to do. That was singularly the worst orgasm, if any orgasm could be bad, I've ever had. She wasn't even experiencing the act with me—more like ordering, using, and then losing interest.

"Don't worry, Andy," she says softly. "It was tolerable."

Tolerable? Did she just call our sex tolerable? I roll away to stare at the ceiling. Shit. I may have blown my one and only chance with her. Maybe I should bring her around with my hand? It's only half past eight; she can't be that tired yet.

Resting a hand on her hip, I savor the smooth softness of her skin. “Carla, honey. Wake up.” A small mew escapes her and her hips rock in a slight movement. Feeling emboldened by her response, I smack her hip lightly.

“Hey! I was getting comfy.” She glances over her shoulder at me. “You can go now.”

The dismissive tone surprises me. “I don’t think so. You haven’t had your turn.” I ease closer to rest against her back while sliding my fingers inward, toward her belly button.

Her bottom leg pressing to the bed lies straight while the top one rests bent at the knee and cocked forward, allowing room to ease down between her slick folds. Her tiny clit still feels aroused, when I flick it softly she moans.

I slide my fingers to bracket the aroused peak, slowly stroking the heated skin next to her clit, mindful of how sensitive the engorged flesh may be. The swollen lips of her sex hug the contours of my thick fingers, causing my cock to stir against her ass.

Keeping my pressure light, I force my pace to stay unhurried. The idea is to build her slowly and then drive her to a huge orgasm. The wet scent of her fills the air and her musky aroma wraps around me.

"Oh...." she whispers while tossing her head on the pillow. Her bare neck lures me and I bow to plant kisses along its length. "Mmm...." Sensing a shift in her, I tilt away allowing her to roll onto her back. Her hard nipples point to the ceiling and her legs spread for easier access.

Carla's eyes are at half-mast, but her movements encourage me to continue. Propped on an elbow, I lean over to capture one peak in my mouth. Laving it with my tongue, a thrill zips through me when she arches to press herself deeper between my lips.

A sigh escapes her and she softly utters, "Johnny..."

"Excuse me?" I don't know who this dream lover is, but I don't intend to stop over a stranger's name. Within a few moments her movements become more energetic, hips gyrating in small tight circles on the bed, her head lashing side to side.

Her eyes snap open and she locks on my face. "Oh, God. Andy, your fingers feel so good."

Her eyes drift back down. I intend to give her pleasure however I can, as long as she's not saying *no*. Sucking one nipple in deep, I nibble the surrounding flesh.

Circling her clit in soft, delicate strokes leaves Carla gulping for breath while her muscles tense. I pull my fingers away from her clit and skim her inner thighs, hoping to make her relax and stop chasing the feelings.

Two or three breaths later she calms down, thrashing less and not holding herself as tight. Reaching to her slit I run two fingers along her wetness, coating them in her arousal. I tickle at her opening to see if I should proceed, when a sexy whimper full of want bubbles from her mouth.

Needing no more proof, I plunge the digits deep and curve them upward, seeking the squishy spot at the top front. Carla arches off the bed, dislodging my mouth from her nipple. I sit up and reach my other hand over to massage her clit again.

"Yes! Yes, just like that!"

Pinching the aroused flesh between my thumb and forefinger, I squeeze lightly, timing her peak. Moisture pours over the fingers lodged inside her as I circle her g-spot, and the moment is right to push her over the finish line.

Carla's eyes open again and she locks onto me, "Andy! Oh my God, I'm gonna come!"

Switching from pinching, I rub her clit hard, steam-rolling past her previous tension in a rocket of sensations. She screams into the dimly lit room and convulses around my hands. Wave after wave of her orgasm washes over her body—a sheer beauty to behold. Especially knowing I gave it to her.

As she quiets, I pull the covers over us and snuggle next to her. She rests her head on my shoulder and I whisper into the darkness, "Was that more than tolerable, Carla?"

"Mmmm...," she says while drifting into sleep.

Chapter Three

Carla

My growling stomach wakes me. When I realize Andrew is still in my bed, an uncomfortable queasiness overshadows the missed meal. Holy hell, what was I thinking? Heather's crazy list at the coffee shop flashes across my mind. She specifically said no *friends with benefits*.

Ugh. Isn't that exactly what I've done *again*, only this time with a co-worker? What the devil was I thinking?

The HR department sent around another reminder about the company's non-dating policy in the office last month. Having never dated a co-worker at this place, it didn't apply to me.

Dated? Ha! You just freakin' slept with the guy.

A shudder hits me hard. Maybe I did cross a line last night. I scoot from under Andy's arm, hopeful I can slip on a robe before he wakes.

No such luck, the second his arm hits the mattress he's alert. "Hey. Where you going?"

I grab the robe hanging on the back of the bathroom door and quickly pull it on. Evidence of our haste to get at each other lays scattered across the room in haphazard droppings of clothes. Andrew's pants lay in a heap and his shirt drapes across the bottom of the bed.

I gather his things into a pile, placing them within his reach.

"Want to get dinner?" he asks, a small, shy smile on his face. "Or maybe order in?"

The knot in my stomach lurches and I force myself to take a deep breath. "This was a mistake."

His face freezes. "What?"

I look toward the door, fidgeting with my robe tie. "It's late. You need to leave. My mom is visiting in the morning."

He runs a hand through his hair and checks the time. "It's barely ten p.m. There are lots of places still delivering. We could share a meal and then I'll head home."

I shake my head and sit on the edge of the bed. Regret over my impulsive actions curves my shoulders, hunching in on myself. “Look, it was fun—but I’m sorry. I don’t date guys from work. Besides, it’s against company policy.”

Andrew grabs his shirt and slips it on. “So, that’s it? Just like that you’re writing me off? Using a convenient excuse like work policy to make it kosher?”

His anger rises, evident in his jerky movements as he finishes dressing. His face is flushed while he slips on his shoes. He stands at the end of the bed facing me. “You won’t use me and blow me off like every other guy. Not this time.”

Shock hits me at his words. Is that what he thinks? That I use and blow off guys? A small niggle in the back of my brain acknowledges I might do exactly what he’s saying. And what does that make me? Not a person I want to be, that’s for damn sure.

I stand to escort him to the door. “It’s not you.” The sex wasn’t all that great so what the hell is the big deal. “It’s me.”

He laughs as he follows me through my apartment. “You’re really using the ‘it’s not you, it’s me’ line? When we didn’t even go on a date? Are you serious?”

I open the door and he stares into my eyes, his body vibrating with energy. “We’re not over, missy.”

I straighten my back and return his bravado. "Yes, we are." I go for the jugular, eager to have my apartment to myself. "It was okay, but I don't intend to experience a repeat performance."

Surprise drops his jaw as I smile and shut the door in his face. Well, that little escapade should make for unwelcome tension in the workplace. Idiot. Heather is right: I've been too casual in choosing my bedmates lately.

A few drinks on an empty stomach and I immediately revert back to unsafe behavior exhibited in college. Time for a change. I'm not that young girl looking for attention or trying to prove myself anymore. I'm a woman who knows what she wants and shouldn't settle for less just because my body has sexual urges.

My stomach growls again, the sickening turmoil I felt earlier disappeared once Andrew left. I help myself to leftovers in the fridge and mentally prepare for the visit with my mother. God, that woman pushes all my buttons. Tomorrow will not be fun.

I take a shower and then drift into bed. The remembrance of Andrew's touch triggers a foggy memory of me writhing on the sheets. Did that bit at the end really happen or was it wishful thinking on my part? The actual act itself was pretty empty so maybe my overactive imagination embellished the new ending.

Thoughts of his blue eyes staring into mine chase me into my dreams.

"Carla, what a great bistro." My mother's voice holds a hint of surprise. Like it's absolutely shocking *I* picked a decent place. "You're lucky they let you in with a blouse that revealing."

First strike. Not as overt as usual. Her opening jab bounces off me and I try to ignore it. She couldn't keep her critical mouth shut for long. I grind my teeth and deliberately tug at the hem of my tight shirt, exposing a tad more cleavage. If she thinks I'm toning down how I dress because she's trying to make me feel sixteen again, then she's got another think coming.

We make it to our table in blessed silence. I order my meal and sip my sweet tea before she starts in on another well-used track.

"Honey, believe me, the kind of men who like flashy women don't last. You'd do better to stop dressing so crass and catch a good one that will last the long haul."

I set down my glass and stare out the window. "Maybe I don't want a man that will last." Why the hell is everyone suggesting I pair up with someone? I might be turning twenty-nine next month, but it's not like I'm a freakin' spinster, for crying out loud.

My comment prompts her to plunge into another disastrous topic. "Good, because none of them will."

Oh, no...I know exactly what's coming next.

"Take a look at your father. He's the best example you'll find on men who run out on a woman."

And there it is. I glance at my watch. Only took two hours to get around to her favorite subject.

"Walked out on us when you were fourteen. Never paid a child support payment, never called—nothing." Her face twists into a bitter mask and pity wells inside me. She never dated after he left. She worked two jobs to make ends meet and keep us together. My younger sister, Julie, never truly missed him; she was too young when he left. But Mom and I both did.

"Yeah, Mom. I know. I was there, too."

"Don't count on a man and you'll be fine."

Our meals arrive and I hold back what's really in my mind. Desperately I want to yell what's been on the tip of my tongue for years: *Right, and look where it's gotten you. You're the unhappiest person I know.*

Instead, I try a different route. "If men are so useless, then why all the grief on my clothes, Mom?"

She harrumphs and picks at her food. "There's no need to look like a tramp, is there?"

Ahh... My mother's conflicting dichotomy of arguments never ceases to amaze me. Thankfully, she's driving back upstate this afternoon.

I smile at the waiter when I catch him eyeing my breasts. He boldly grins before heading to another table.

My mother gasps. "Dear God, you're not thinking about picking up the waiter are you? Surely you've got better sense than that?" She shakes her head, disbelief marring her face. "If you're going to live your life as a 'good time' girl at least be smart enough to pick a guy with money."

I feel the emotional wall between us growing a little bit stronger and higher. Why did I agree to her visit today? Oh yeah, her birthday's next week.

I remain quiet during the rest of the meal, half listening as she once more lists all the ways to avoid unhappiness in my life. Too bad she never has any advice that could actually *help* her daughters.

At three o'clock I'm eager to send my mother on her way. As she climbs into her car, I dutifully kiss her cheek and deliver the empty promise that we'll get together again soon. My muscles feel weak and drained after holding my opinions inside for so long.

She's got to be the most miserable person I've ever met. Is it any wonder her two extroverted daughters don't race to spend time with her? That kind of negativity sucks the positive energy out of a person.

Back at my apartment, I change into jeans and a t-shirt and head out to *Dress for Success*. It's my turn to log in donated clothes that arrive on a Saturday. The trip across town helps to wash away the inadequate feelings my mother never fails to stir.

Melissa waves from the front desk when I enter, her chipper smile and calm personality a great match for welcoming newcomers. The organization provides nice, gently used business outfits to low-income women re-entering the workforce. A lot of these ladies remind me of my mother all those years ago, with one major exception—most of them aren't bitter man-haters.

They may be single moms, newly divorced women with no kids, or married ladies attempting to change careers after earning a diploma at night, but all of them come with a sense of hope. Something my mom has lacked since the day Dad left.

In my teens, I often wondered what happened to him, but gave up the hope of him returning long before becoming an adult.

"Carla?" Cindy calls, pulling me from my negative thoughts. Cindy is the tall blonde who handles new arrivals at *Dress for Success*. "Peggy had to leave and someone's here who needs to pick out a suit. Care to help?"

I smile, happy to do my favorite task rather than unload clothes. "You bet." I cross the lobby to shake hands with the young Hispanic woman next to Cindy.

"This is Erica," Cindy introduces us. "Erica, Carla is the best personal shopper we've got. She'll have you dressed like a million bucks in no time."

I gesture for Erica to follow me and we make our way to the rack-filled room that never fails to bring a smile to the candidates who seek help from the program.

A small gasp sounds from behind me. "I feel like I've died and gone to clothing heaven."

Joy bubbles inside me as I turn to the young woman. A large smile creases my face as I look Erica over from head to toe. "Are you about a size ten?" She nods. "Great. I know we've got something that will work for you. Where are you interviewing?"

The latter part of my day outweighed the crappy encounter with my mother. It's after six by the time I get home and for once, I don't mind not having a date lined up. It'll be nice to chill for a night and forget about men for a while.

You mean forget about Andy, don't you? Wasn't it his blue eyes you were mooning over while unpacking clothes?

No, it was not. I mean all men.

Uh-huh. Sure.

I flop on the couch, pushing thoughts of last night from my mind, and finally check my phone—an act which done at lunch would have unloaded a shit storm of remarks from my mother on my bad manners. There are several texts from Heather, offering encouragement, as she knew I was meeting my mom today. And one from Andrew. *I want to see you again.*

I return Heather's texts first. Thanking her for her pep talk and then I keep my return texts bitching about my mom to a minimum.

I debate on what to say to Andrew. Might as well be blunt and get it over with. *Not going to happen.*

He immediately texts back. *It can be good between us. Give me another chance.*

My face heats in embarrassment as his words remind me of the crass "it was tolerable" comment I made after we had sex. I can't believe I said such a shitty thing! Not one of my finer moments. Although, the experience wasn't anything to write home about.

What should I say to convince him to leave me alone and realize this thing between us isn't going anywhere? If I make the response too harsh, I'm a bitch. Too light and teasing, he'll think he has a chance. And his chances of a rematch of last night are slim to none.

No thanks. I don't date guys at work.

We're not exactly dating.

Exasperation leaves me in a sigh at his deliberate obtuseness. *I don't sleep with guys at work. Is that more clear?*

Yup. I won't sleep with you at work. Got it.

Not interested. Good night, Andrew. With a growl, I shut off my phone for the night.

Chapter Four
Andrew

Dammit! That little minx just brushed me off! I click my phone to sleep and slam it on the coffee table. Man, I knew I should've trusted my gut and not slept with her. She's going to use that stupid *no dating at work policy* to shut me out—which I know she wouldn't have used had I been on my game when we had sex.

One chance! I had one chance with her and I blew it! Is she even going to acknowledge I'm the one who pleasured her afterward or is her sleep-fogged brain crediting it to her mysterious dream lover? Hell, she called out my name and seemed fully aware of her faculties. Maybe the alcohol helped her forget.

No. She wasn't that far gone. And you know it. She just doesn't want you.

I've admired Carla from afar too long. Now that I've seen the passion simmering below her surface, I aim to draw it out, stroke it to life, and leave it begging for more —*from me*. Not some dream lover she calls out by mistake. Damn, that really rubbed me raw. A woman's never done that before.

She needs a man like me—a man with a gentle hand who won't tolerate her mindless flirting, and who will keep her sexually satisfied, to never *need* to wander to another man's bed. Turning her around to monogamous sex will be an incredible challenge. One I am mightily looking forward to.

What is it about the prickly lady that draws me? Is it the hurt beneath the bravado? I bet someone messed with that girl's head for years. I'd like nothing more than to kiss her senseless and drive every thought of other men from her mind forever.

My doorbell rings. It's Rocko from across the hall. "Hey, Ace." He greets me with his usual fist bump then a half-hug, shoulder touch with a brief clap on the back preferred by a lot of touchy-feely musician types. "You watching the game?"

The scruffy appearance of my neighbor pulls a smile from me. Instead of the leather vest he performs in, he's wearing old flannel and jeans. His adoring fans should see him now.

"Sure, want to join me?"

"Yeah, that'd be great." He runs a hand across his scraggly beard. "Tonight's gig was cancelled, so I'm staying in."

"What, no hot date with a groupie?"

"Come on, man. You know that shit gets old once you hit thirty. Like I'm molesting a bunch of barely legal college girls."

I grab us some beers, settle on the couch, and turn on the game. We drink in silence for a few moments, watching the players warm up by throwing a ball around the bases.

"Did you play last night?" I ask. Rocko is lead guitar in a local band. They're working hard, playing any gig they can in the hopes of building a fan base to catapult their song sales.

He nods, his eyes on the game. "Tiny hole in the wall—Fitzpatrick's—right here in the Village. Great crowd."

"Yeah, I've been there before. Good energy."

We watch the game together, but my mind keeps wandering. I need to figure out a way to seduce Carla back into bed, to prove I can be the kind of lover she's looking for.

Does she even know what the hell she's looking for?

I shake my head at my silent musings, not really sure where I messed up things last night, but determined not to quit.

"Dude?" Rocko asks.

"Huh?" Damn, has he been talking to me for a while?

"You've got that far off look on your face again. Is it over that chick at work you mentioned?"

"Am I that obvious?" I laugh. "I saw Carla on Friday."

"It's pretty easy." He smiles. "You look all stupid-spacey and shit." He coughs into his hand to pretend to hide his next word: "Pussy." I glare at him across the couch. He shrugs, uncaring. "How did it go?"

My chest tightens in frustration. "Let's just say it was not my finest performance."

He laughs, his humor at my expense filling the room. "Dude, you messed up? Oh, that's rich. You can charm the panties off ladies of all ages the moment your fingers tickle the ivories." He gestures to the baby grand sitting in what would be my apartment's dining area. "And yet in an office environment you tank?" He snorts. "That's fucking pathetic."

I ignore him and take a swig from my beer. My silence is the male equivalent of stating I refuse to rise to his bait.

"So," Rocko says, "what do you plan to do? Gonna give up like a wuss?"

"No," I bite out, surprised by the vehemence in my tone. "I just need a plan. Something that will get her thinking about me..."

"Remember that Tina chick I dated a couple of years ago?"

A vague memory of him mentioning a Tina stirs in the depths of my brain. "I think so. What about her?"

"She came across as rough on the outside, but was a hellcat in bed." A satisfied smirk tugs the corner of his mouth. "Man, she brought out the wild in me. Really liked it when I came on strong."

"Yeah, so?"

"She turned off every guy with her smart ass comments and sneer." He picks at the label on his beer. "But under that do-not-touch exterior was one hot tamale."

"What happened to this hot woman? Why did you let her go?"

"Not me, man. She moved for work." He takes a long drink from his beer. "If a gig ever takes me to Baltimore, I'll be looking her up."

We lapse into quiet and I wonder if Carla could be like Tina. Maybe she'd like me to come on strong. I watch more of the game, lost in thought.

The mental pull from the shiny piano nags at the back of my brain. I'd like nothing better than to lose myself in the feel of the keys beneath my fingers and the sound of the notes filling the air. But this complex woman keeps drifting into my head, demanding my attention.

She's a complicated bird, Carla. Haven't quite figured her out yet. Likes to flirt with everyone—which could just be a natural part of her personality and that's made her a good salesperson. If I'm honest, perhaps it's more that she's very approachable and friendly instead of an outright flirt.

I take another long drink, the cool amber liquid easing the tightness in my chest. On the other hand, I have witnessed her leave with a guy from the bar, so her behavior does go beyond flirting when she wants. One other thing I've noticed—I never hear her mention her latest hook-up at work. That usually means the man isn't in the picture anymore. Watching her for the past few months has shown me more into her psyche than she might like.

Tension radiated off her last night after mentioning her mother. And yet in the brief exchanges we had tonight in texts she didn't say anything about the woman. *That's because she was too busy trying to blow you off, jackass.*

No, I don't think that's it. In the short personal conversations we've shared since we met, she's casually mentioned a sister, her best friend Heather, and where she grew up. Nothing about her folks. I wonder why.

A fist clenches in my chest when I think of my own parents. After Dad died a few years ago, Mom has gone downhill. The hospice nurse said she may pass any day now. I'm going to go see her again tomorrow, even though my sister has been there every day.

Acceptance settles through me at the realization our mother's fight will finally come to an end. This two-year battle has been draining—for her, my sister, and me. We both said our goodbyes when our mom was still cognizant of her surroundings. Since then all we can do is keep her comfortable. The frustration I felt over her imminent death released its hold a while ago—and not a moment too soon. I wouldn't want anything to taint a peaceful passing for her.

Rocko and I watch the next few innings in silence, one of us venturing to the kitchen for a fresh beer every so often. An alarm goes off on my watch.

"I'm going to call my mom. Do you mind?"

Rocko grabs the remote and mutes the sound, familiar with my nightly ritual. "Nah. Go ahead, man."

I finish my beer and shove the guilt of missing my call last night to the back of my mind. My mother would've never wanted me to feel bad or obligated, and I've got to keep that forefront in my mind so I can enjoy this last bit of time with her.

I move toward my first love and sit on the cushioned bench, setting my fingers to the keys like I've done for over twenty years. I work through scales, warming up, and launch into one of my mother's favorite Elton songs, *Candle in the Wind.* The music fills the apartment, bouncing back to fill my soul with warmth. The words spill out, freeing all the heart and passion I lock up at work every damn day to earn a steady paycheck to pay medical bills.

Rocko raises his beer in tribute, but remains silent, focused on the game.

When I'm done, I call the nurse on duty. "Hi, Iris. How's she doing?"

"Same as yesterday. No change."

"Thanks. Do you mind holding the phone for her?"

"Not at all, child. I love to hear your voice."

I set the cell phone on the piano lid and begin to play.

Chapter Five

Carla

Sundays always whip past too soon. The only good thing about yesterday was getting chores done, like laundry, and not having to field more texts from Andrew. At least he took the hint Saturday night.

A tiny twinge of disappointment swells inside me and I squash it. I want to be alone. I don't need a man in my life to make me happy.

Yeah, and you're such a joy to be around the rest of the time.

I feel a growl bubbling in my throat and stifle it. Damn, if I could just find a decent guy to sleep with, I wouldn't be so freakin' on edge all the time. Used to be I'd spend an evening with one of my many battery powered nightstand buddies and I'd be right as rain. But, the past six months haven't been the same. Add in the fact every freakin' guy I've tried has been a disappointment in the sack. No wonder I'm a little tense.

Tense? Is that another word for bitchy and hard up?

No! It's just tense. Don't read in more than it is.

Uh-huh. Sure.

I finish the last touches on my makeup, sweep a fine powder over it to set, and then gather the rest of my things for work. Andrew's help on the Stringer account means I'm starting my day by meeting the owner before heading into the office.

The meeting goes well. Jennifer is a bubbling cauldron of ideas and energy. She's the most ambitious and hard-working woman I've ever met. I present some new suggestions for exposure and we hammer out the details together. When I leave her office, the high of success buoys me the entire trip to Smith and White. I love my job. It's always a challenge and never boring.

I arrive in the office at ten; the rest of the staff is well into their morning. I keep my eyes down as I head to my cubicle, eager to avoid Andrew's penetrating gaze as long as possible. Heat fills my cheeks over Friday night's antics. God, what was I thinking inviting a guy from work to my place?

Biggest mistake ever.

I settle my belongings and fire up my laptop. Within minutes I'm logged into the company server and skimming emails. One from Andrew catches my eye.

Do I open it? I doubt he'd act like an idiot at work, so I might as well see what he has to say.

How did the meeting go with Jennifer Stringer?

Relief pours through me at his professional inquiry. Maybe we can pretend Friday night didn't happen. That would make my life sOoOoOooo much easier.

I send him back a short note. *Good, thanks. I'll be working with the design team closely this week to finalize the pitch on the next campaign.*

Want to share lunch to chat about details?

Dammit. I knew he'd leap to something personal.

No. Thank you.

I fire off the last email, then collect the files I need to copy for the designers. Maybe in a few days he'll stop trying so hard and we can return to the way things were between us. Professional and slightly distant. Just the way I like it.

Yeah, because that's worked so well for you before.

The hum of the copier distracts me from my thoughts of Andrew. Once one section of the Stringer file is done, I place it back into the tabs and start with the next.

"Hey, Carla," Andrew calls from behind me.

I glance to see him leaning against the doorframe, and he tosses me a hopeful smile. God, it was hell waking up with him in my bed. After a slip up during my first internship nine years ago, I vowed to never do anything so stupid again.

"Hi," I turn to my task.

"We still haven't talked about our night together. How long do you intend to put me off?"

Forever? Damn, I was afraid this would happen. Holding in the heavy sigh longing to escape, I face my pushy co-worker. "No offense, but I'm not interested in dating an accountant."

"Excuse me?" His tone comes out sharper than I've ever heard from him. "Do you think I'm not worthy of you because of *my job*?"

"Umm... no. Sorry." That's exactly it, but saying so is bitchier than I'd like. I switch to the next file and give him my back. "Listen, it was a fun night and all, but I want more excitement. Something spicy."

His footsteps behind me are barely audible over the hum of the copier. Hands rest on my hips and I tense.

"You have no idea what you want. You could have excitement right in front of you and you wouldn't know what to do about it."

Annoyed, I whip around to face him, dislodging his hands. "Really? And you think I don't remember the tolerable three minutes we shared?"

His deep blue eyes darken in anger and he leans closer, crowding my space. "I think you recall someone named Johnny and seem to be attributing some of our time together to a dream about him."

A blush creeps up my cheeks, I do remember having dreamed about an old college flame, but how the hell does he know that? "Umm... I..."

"You called out his name," his warm breath tickles my lips, "while I pleasured you."

Startled by the revelation, I dart to the side and make for the door. "I don't know what you're talking about."

His voice whispers when the copier cycles down, "You're sexy when you let down your guard."

I turn to face him. He takes two quick strides and captures my mouth. His lips press against mine and a coil of heat unravels in my middle. A warm hand caresses the back of my head, gently drawing me closer.

I open my mouth to protest and his tongue slips inside to spar with my own. The rush of blood pounding through my veins brings a tingly feeling that halts my words before they form. His wide open eyes stare into my own, challenging me with the heat I see simmering in their depths.

His mouth tastes like fresh coffee heavily laced with cream. My knees weaken at the intensity and warmth pouring off him. He nibbles on my bottom lip and a spike of pleasure jolts down my spine, jarring me from the spell he's weaving.

I place two hands on his chest and push him away. Our lips break and a shudder runs through me. "What the hell was that?" My tone sounds indignant, but my body betrays me with arousal.

Andy smiles, a slow, indulgent curve of his lips. His tongue slips out to run along his full mouth. "I think you know exactly what that was." He boldly reaches out a hand and runs a finger over my right nipple, peaked hard and pressing against the inside of my bra.

I swat his hand away.

"It's passion, Carla. Don't fight it."

I take a step back, putting distance between us and regain my composure. "You do that again and I'll report you."

Andy steps closer, crowding my space. "No, you won't."

A sneer forms on my face. "Oh, really? And why wouldn't I?"

"Because I know what you need, darling. And I aim to give it to you."

His confidence and arrogance rocks me. This is a side of Andy I never knew existed. "Go pound salt, bastard." I storm out of the copier room, wrapping my indignation around me like a cape. Andy's amused chuckle follows me down the hall.

Son of a bitch. I'll be damned if I'm corralled into a torrid affair at work. No matter what my body tells me.

Crap! I left the files in there. I'm not going back to get them until he leaves. Call me a chicken, but I'm not ready to face him again.

It's Wednesday, and I've done my best to avoid Andrew the past two days. When office emails went around about getting a drink after hours, I almost didn't agree to go. I wasn't sure if Andrew was going or how to handle him. The memory of his stolen kiss has haunted me.

The lingering heat stirred from his bold advance left me tossing and turning in bed each night. Twice I tried to seek relief on my own, and twice I was left frustrated and horny. Damn him! I will not date a guy from work. It's career suicide.

I run a finger through the condensation on my wine glass and contemplate what to do. The energy in the crowded bar wraps around me in a familiar feeling—the hotspot is always packed. This time, I'm careful not to get drunk and don't sit near Andrew. God, he's like a puppy sniffing after me. I have no intention of winding up with him. I want an exciting man.

And how do you know that man isn't Andy?

Because I won't let it be, dammit! I know what I want and he's not it. Temporary, hot sex is easier—and he seems to be gunning for more than I'm willing to offer.

I grab my drink in anger, but wisely take only a sip. I have no desire to muddle my senses with Andrew staring at me across the bar. Why the hell does he like me anyway? I've stated I'm not interested. I've brought out my most bitchy self, and he still keeps coming.

He needs to see me pick up another guy. That should wipe away that smug look I see every time I glance over at him. Thinks he's got my number, does he? I'll show him.

Tall, broad-shouldered, and beautiful walks into my field of vision. The big man looks vaguely familiar, so I smile.

"Well hello, sweetheart. I remember you from last week." He returns my interest with a crooked grin and looks around. He notes Andrew sitting a few stools away. "You look more stable tonight."

Ah, yes. He's the guy I fell into when trying to leave last week. "Hi." I tilt my head, allowing my hair to frame my face. "And you look just as nice as you did when we first met. Do you work in the area?"

"Yeah. I'm in finance—stocks and bonds mostly. You?"

"Advertising sales exec at Smith and White."

A feral look sparks in his eye and I wonder if he could be what I'm looking for.

"Want to go catch some dinner at a quieter place?" Tall and handsome asks.

"I'd love to."

We leave the bar together and I can almost feel Andrew's annoyance radiating toward us. That'll show him once and for all I'm not interested.

Chapter Six

Andrew

I cannot believe that little tease left with that meathead! My hands clench into fists and I have to physically press them under the edge of the bar to stop myself from chasing after her. Why does she go for the hulking, empty-headed guys? Why won't she look at me with interest?

I take a deep breath and will the logical part of my brain into working. Maybe because she can control them easier than she can me? After our night together I haven't exactly reverted to the calm and easy-going guy she used to work with. Her response when I pleasured her is still etched in my mind. She reacted to my advances with an uninhibited sweetness; almost like her body was surprised she enjoyed it.

The bossy, confident woman she presents to the world is not all that meets the eye with Carla. If she were secure in herself, why would she pick up strangers at a bar? I've seen it enough in my time as a musician—a lonely person looking for companionship, often making unwise choices for human contact.

Could that be true with her, too? And if yes, how do I convince her I'm worth more than a one night stand?

More importantly, why do you care? Why are you willing to take a risk on a woman who just figuratively thumbed her nose at you in public?

Because there's something about her… something that calls to me. Is it the vulnerability I saw in her eyes when we kissed in the copier room? Is it the freedom she only allows herself when she's sleepy and her guard is down? She acts like she's in charge, but I bet what she really needs is for the man to take control for a change.

I throw my money on the bar and make the journey to my apartment. I knock twice on Rocko's door to see if he's in. A muffled "Yo!" comes from within. In a moment the door flies open and my neighbor stands bare-chested before me, wearing sweatpants.

"Dude." Rocko says, drawing out the word in a long greeting. "I'm going to the gym. Want to come?"

The tension growing inside me from watching Carla walk out with another guy needs an outlet. "Sounds good. I'll meet you downstairs in five."

Rocko nods and shuts his door.

I quickly change and meet him in the building's small basement gym. It's nothing pretty, and the cramped space filled with old free weights is near the laundry room, but it gets the job done for a free work out.

About forty-five minutes into our chest and back rotation Rocko says, "You going to tell me what's eating you or do you plan on giving yourself an aneurism with the extra weight?"

Sweat drips from my forehead as I push the bar to the top notch of the frame. I slide the weight into the start position, expelling air in a whoosh at the effort. I grab the hand towel I brought and mop the moisture from my eyes.

"Little minx picked up a guy at the bar after work. Right in front of me."

"Damn." Rocko whistles. "That's harsh. Didn't try coming on strong, like I suggested?"

"I did. But maybe I wasn't clear enough."

I rise, wipe the bench free of my sweat, and then stand behind the bar to spot Rocko on his set.

"She's sent *you* a clear message she's not interested, man." He wraps his hands around the bar and hesitates. "Take off twenty from both ends." He smirks. "I don't have any issues to sweat out like you."

"Fine," I grumble before removing the weights.

Rocko watches while I return the weights to the stationary rack behind us. "So, what do you plan to do?"

I shake my head and return to my spotter position. Rocko lifts the bar and starts his set. "I'm thinking I need to get right in her face and *show* her what I can do to her body, make her respond to me before she talks herself out of it."

Rocko remains silent, concentrating on his form and breathing. At the end he pushes the bar into its starting position. "As long as whatever you're planning won't get a restraining order against you, I say go for it. You only live once, right?" His face grimaces. "Sorry man, that slipped out. How is your mom doing?"

I wave him off. I know he didn't mean anything by his comment, and I don't want anyone on eggshells around me. "No change. Still in a coma. They think she could go any day now." A sigh rushes out, and the last of my tension leaves with it. "It's a crappy situation all around, but we knew it was leading to this."

We select dumbbells and start a round of flys on the incline benches. "How's Andrea holding up?" Rocko wiggles his eyebrows, possibly hoping to interject some lightness into the conversation. "Does she need a comforting shoulder or manly hug?"

His distraction works and a sharp bark of laughter erupts from me. "Man, don't go near my sister. I'll have to hurt you."

"Come on, Ace...she's so pretty." Sweat runs down his face as he winks at me. "You sure she's related to you?"

We finish our workout and part ways. I still feel keyed up and debate on a run, deciding against it at the last minute and shower instead. The entire time I'm walking through the motions of bathing and then fixing a meal, I contemplate Carla and what to do. She wants something spicy in her life, does she?

I've got just what she needs. I change into jeans and a polo then head back out to the bar. Here's to hoping she falls for my plan.

Chapter Seven

Carla

Two hours after leaving the bar, I can barely nod my head politely while Tall- Handsome-and-Dumb speaks. He might be pretty, but I have no desire to take him home. I politely exit after our meal, pleading an early morning meeting and files I need to review. Brian and I exchange numbers, but I doubt very highly either of us will call. The chemistry isn't there.

Didn't have that problem with Andy, did you?

Could I be wrong and there really is something between us that could spark the sheets on fire? I push the thought aside and refuse to linger on the idea. Counting on any man is a mistake, and one I intend to avoid.

Pretty soon I'm home alone, snuggled up with comfy clothes, a cup of hot tea, and ready to start a book Heather recommended called *Suddenly Beautiful*. Last week, she raved about the paranormal story and the hysterical antics of the heroine. I gamely agreed to give it a shot.

A few chapters in, I'm so fully engrossed I don't glance at the screen when I pick up my ringing phone.

"Hello?"

"Carla, it's me." Andy's voice comes over the line, slightly distorted by background noise.

A sigh escapes me. I really can't handle drama tonight. I hear the bitchiness coming out in my voice before I rein it in. "What is it, Andy?"

"I need you to meet me at the bar. I want to talk to you about the Stringer account."

"Seriously? Can't we just talk on the phone?"

"No," he says, and hangs up.

Bastard! He better not be playing a game or I am so going to report his ass at the office. With the recent increase in the campaign budget, I could request to work with another accountant. The idea fizzles the moment it comes. They'd never switch him off the account without a very good reason. And I don't have one, *yet*. I'd never report his flirting, especially after I slept with him. Being a bitch to chase him away is one thing, messing with his career is another.

I debate on changing out of my yoga clothes and decide against it. Not like I'm going to impress anyone. I run my fingers through my short hair and head out.

Sure, and you're fluffing your hair to make sure you look good for who...?

Ignoring my inner voice of obviousness I continue to the bar.

Sexually frustrated from my aborted evening with Brian, I scan the packed establishment for my co-worker. "Question on the account, my ass. Where is he?" Grabbing my cell, I dial his number.

"Carla?" His voice sounds softer than the noise of the bar around me.

"Yeah. Where are you?"

"I'm in the back, down the hall. It's quieter here."

"Fine. I'll come to you." Pressing my way through the throng, I make it to the dark hall leading to the bathrooms. "Andy?" A hot hand latches onto my arm and pulls me into a side storage room. "What the hell are you doing?"

"You want something spicy, and I'm giving it to you." A strip of dark cloth covers my eyes and I'm pressed against a shelving rack. Rough movements tie the material at the back of my head and a hard body presses into mine from behind. “You’ve been a bad girl, Carla.”

Excitement cascades up my spine, but I’ll be damned if I tell him.

“What the fuck are you talking about? Let me go or I’m going to scream.”

“Oh, you’ll scream, all right,” he plants a soft kiss on my neck, “but not in fear or anger.” Hands reach around and grab my breasts over my snug cotton top. Despite what I keep telling myself about this frustrating man, my body responds and my nipples tighten.

“Not funny, you bastard.” I’m uncomfortable with the power this exciting moment holds over me. “Look, I know you’re not a rapist. You should stop before you do something illegal.”

Clever fingers twist my hardened peaks through the lace covering them, drawing a gasp from me.

“I know what you need, Carla.”

“Really? If you did you’d be letting me go, right now. I don’t like this kind of shit.”

My shirt slides up and cool air tickles my exposed flesh. “Hah!” his voice barks out, rough with desire. “You don’t know what you like. You fumble with the wrong men and think commanding them will get you what you need.”

His comment strikes too close to reality, especially after I shouted orders at him during our brief encounter. Grasping fingers have worked the cups of my bra down, and stretch my elongated aroused nipples.

The inability to see him touching me feels freeing. Like the experience is not quite happening to me. Moisture gathers in my panties, and despite my complaints, I can't deny this is turning me on.

"Andy—"

"Shh... Don't say a word. Just *feel* for a few minutes." He removes his hands from my breasts and guides me to hold onto one of the shelves I'm pressed against. "If you are afraid and don't want me to continue, say so and I'll stop."

My yoga pants are pushed down around my knees, and strong hands guide my bottom to tilt out, on display. He rubs the exposed skin, while waiting for me to answer. Not knowing what will come next and being open to other senses feels...arousing—and not just physically.

Big hands massage my backside, sparking gooseflesh in the air-conditioned space. The heavy storage room door muffles the noise of the bar and the dust tickles my nose. Cold steel under my hand and the trapped feeling of my pants around my knees invigorate me.

"Well, Carla? Are you ready to live a little? Silence is your acceptance."

Anticipation tightens every muscle in my body. For once I'm speechless. Do I protest or give it a try? The blindfold makes me feel safe, unexposed. I bow my head slightly, unaware if he sees my actions, but I know what I'm doing.... I'm accepting. The rubbing on my bottom ceases and the cool air rises goose bumps.

Whack! Andy's hand slaps my right ass cheek.

"Ow!"

Smack! Another blow lands on the left cheek. "Shhh... you speak and I'll spank you."

"That's—"

Smack!

The sting from his firm hand sends a thrill up my spine. He's not hitting to cause damage. Just hard enough to get my attention and show he means it. Heat races to the enflamed skin and a blossom of sensation spreads.

The tingle creeps to my wet center, alerting me to the throbbing in my clit. Each pulse of blood pumping to my punished flesh sends a jolt of arousal to the little bud as well.

"You've been naughty, Carla. Picking up men in bars." His warm palm caresses my stinging butt, fingers curving around the firm globes, reaching in toward my thong-covered crotch.

"Oh yes, that's right—"

Three hard slaps follow, rapid fire, leaving me gasping.

"Quiet. Control yourself and then you'll get pleasure."

Wiggling my ass, I silently beg for one of the soothing caresses to smooth the pain away. I never thought I'd be one to like spanking, but the stinging slaps make me feel alive. More alive than I have in years.

"Very good." His voice oozes like honey in the darkness. "You like that, don't you?"

Afraid to speak and feel his hand again, I nod my head, hoping he's looking. The cocooning blackness of the blindfold releases me from worrying about my body—how I'll look, how he looks...and makes me *feel* everything. When he reaches beneath my panties and probes my slick folds, a whimper of want escapes.

Tension fills me—could the sound count as speaking? Will he spank me again? I can't decide if I want another smack or not.

Apparently the whimper doesn't count; he continues to push a thick finger into me. Steadily, he pumps in and out as I struggle to remain still. The elastic straining around my spread knees allows a few inches of space between my thighs. I rise onto my tiptoes, trying to tilt my bottom back for better penetration.

One hand on my hip pushes me down, lowering my feet flat to the storage room floor. "No, Carla, you let me decide what you feel or I'll leave you hanging."

Outrage heats my face, would he really do that? "No!"

Slap, slap, slap! "Shush, baby, or you'll never get there."

Annoyance courses through me as the sting in my ass settles down. Who in the hell does he think he is? If I want to come then I should be able to do whatever the hell I want to get myself there. A second finger plunges into my depths, stretching me and pumping faster. The hand on my hip reaches around and rubs my clit through the cotton crotch of my underwear.

All of my anger fades as a small circling starts. "More," I say.

Wet fingers pull from inside me.

Smack!

The hardest slap yet. Five more follow quickly and tears sting my eyes. The circling pressure on my clit doesn't stop the entire time, it increases, pushing me higher and into a wild state of frenzy.

Soft moans and whimpers spill from my lips and I worry he's never going to put those fingers back in. A short caress of his hand soothes where he spanked and then he sinks two fingers into me.

"I'll tell you when to come. And you're going to cream over my hands when you do." His soft voice sounds just above a whisper, sending a chill racing down my back. "I know what you need, Carla."

Desperate to hold myself as still as possible, I clench the shelf as another gasp escapes me. A third finger stabs into my depths, driving me higher and closer to the brink.

"You want it, baby. I feel your muscles inside gripping my fingers." The hand working my clit stops circling and pulls the fabric roughly to the side. "Just like if my cock were working you deep." Light pats to the aroused flesh pulls my focus from his plunging fingers.

"Uh... uh..." Low guttural noises reach my ears, foreign sounding and far away. Good God, they may be coming from me. Pleasure spirals up my spine to course through my body and I bite down to clamp the begging word *please* from spilling into the night.

"That's it, Carla. You're ready now."

Rubbing starts on my clit again and the sensations rocket from my crotch in wave after wave of tingles. A scream bubbles forth and echoes back in the small room.

"Come for me, baby." Desire pours from me, coating his hand like he said. The pumping continues and my orgasm drags on and on, wringing the very life from me.

Collapsing forward, I catch myself by locking my elbows for support. The blindfold at my head is loosened and stars fill my vision. Tender hands adjust my underwear and pull my pants and shirt into place.

Andy wraps himself around my back and wedges his face near my neck. "Consider that your first lesson."

Chapter Eight

Andrew

My phone rings as I'm getting ready for work. A slow smile creeps across my face as I reach for it, hoping it's Carla. She refused to come to my place last night and practically ran out of the bar as fast as she could. My musings stop cold when I see the call is from the nursing home caring for my mom.

"Your mom's condition has worsened. We think you should come see her today if you can."

Pressure fills my chest as I grip the phone. "I'll be there within the hour."

I call work to schedule a personal day and then dial my sister, Andrea. She answers on the first ring. “Did they call you, too?” she asks in lieu of a greeting.

“Yeah, I was about to leave. Want to go together?”

“I’ll swing by and pick you up.”

Twenty minutes later and we’re driving to the home in Brooklyn. “Talk to me, Andrea.” I close my fingers over her hand, squeezing it briefly before letting go. “How are you doing with all of this?”

A heavy sigh escapes my sister. “As good as can be expected, I guess.” She takes her eyes off the road to glance at me quickly, the bright blue orbs piercing in their intensity. “It’s not like we didn’t know this was coming.”

Once more, I grasp her hand on the gearshift, grateful I’ve got her by my side, not dealing with mom’s situation on my own. “She’ll be with Dad soon.”

We spend the rest of the day at the facility, alternating between sitting at our mom’s bedside and double checking the paperwork to make sure her wishes will be met when she passes. She and my father even picked out their headstone together. If there were ever a more pragmatic and loving couple, I’ve never seen one.

In a way, watching them as we grew up was a blessing and a curse. Andrea and I never doubted we were loved—our parents were older when they underwent fertility treatments—but we witnessed such a powerful connection between a married couple that we could never settle for less in our own lives.

I've wondered if searching for what they shared has kept my headstrong sister single all these years. She may be a pain in the ass at times, but she's still an amazing woman.

Even though I'm here with Andrea and our mom, my thoughts drift to Carla. I'd like nothing more than to call, just to hear her voice. Whether or not she'd be happy to hear from me is another story altogether. We're not there yet. And I don't know if we ever will be.

I've watched her for months, slowly falling for the headstrong woman so like my sister. Carla has a softer side, too, one she doesn't let out much. But I've seen it nonetheless.

I've witnessed her race from the office when her friends needed her. I've heard her on the phone with the charity she feels so strongly about. I forwarded the email she mistakenly sent to me for donations to my sister who happily sent some older suits to the cause. I've seen her return from a yoga session during lunch, with the inner glow of contentment shining from every pore.

She's like a spiky durian fruit: her thorny exterior hiding all the sweetness within. Sweetness no other man but me has taken the time to notice. If they had, they wouldn't have given up after one round with the bossy hellion.

Carla has ignored my casual advances for months, and rather than put me off, her behavior has intrigued me further. No woman has mentally challenged me as much.

As I sit here next to my dying mother, one of her favorite sayings comes to me, "Anything worth having in life requires hard work." Our parents encouraged us to follow our dreams, to never be afraid of failure, and to never give up on what we wanted most.

The doctor came in a little while ago and assured us she is holding steady, out of the worst part of this recent decline. We can leave and not worry she'll pass in our absence. But they did advise us to stay in town to be easily reached when her condition changed.

I lean forward and kiss my mom's forehead. The waiting is awful, but I know she'll soon find peace in my father's arms.

The car ride home is quiet, each of us mulling over our own thoughts. Soon we're minutes from my building and I realize I don't want today with my sister to end. "Want to go to an early dinner? I'd like to hear about your work."

Andrea shrugs, the gesture somehow elegant on her. "Work is work, up and down at best. Got an article coming up about the rise in education for women through online courses." Andrea started out of college as a journalist and now writes independent pieces for various online news reporting agencies.

"Good for you. Steady work is all that matters."

Her mouth contorts into a grimace. "I'm sorry I haven't been able to contribute more for Mom's care."

I glance out the window, hoping we can find a place to park. "We're getting by fine. Don't worry so much."

"You say that... but you're the only one sacrificing your dreams. It just kills me."

"If music paid the bills I'd be happier, sure, but I'll get back to it eventually. This accounting gig isn't permanent." I motion out the window. "There's a spot, grab it."

My sister maneuvers her old Honda into the tight parking space. "It certainly seems like it after two years. I don't know what we would have done if we had to pay the medical bills on what I make as a writer." She looks at me and smiles, "Probably have to start consolidating expenses, like moving in together."

A shudder runs through me at the thought of living with my perpetually messy twin. “Hey, now, let’s not get hasty.”

She laughs as we exit the car. “Wouldn’t want me to cramp your musician lifestyle?”

I think of Rocko standing at his doorway last month, a mid-twenties bar groupie hanging on his tattooed arm while he tried to give the woman the polite shove off the morning after a gig. Do I miss the one-night stands? I shake my head while joining my sister on the sidewalk. I outgrew those empty encounters years ago.

“Not at all. More worried your slovenly habits would push me to kill you in your sleep.” She shoves me hard, laughing the whole time. “Let’s go inside,” I say, motioning to the closest restaurant. “I’m hungry.”

Chapter Nine

Carla

Andy wasn't at work today. I tossed and turned all night, trying to figure out what I should do and how I should approach him, only to find the effort was all in vain. I'm curious why he's out of the office, but still uncertain on how to act. If I text him, he'll think I care and I'm not sure it's a good idea to open that can of worms again.

But you are starting to care, you idjit. The passion he stirred in you last night was explosive.

I squirm in my chair, unable to deny how exciting our escapade in the storage room was. Where did he learn to do that? Does he spank women all the time? Damn, it was hot. Probably the wildest thing I've done in my life and I thought I was pretty damn wild already.

Screwing lots of men doesn't make you wild. It makes you easy.

Freakin' hell. Is that what I've done? Slept with a lot of men with nothing to show for it? No mind-blowing orgasms, no satisfied sleep, no fond memories of men I'd like to encounter again? Damn, I really have made a mess of my life.

I'm grateful Heather agreed to dinner after work. I need someone sane to talk to. I'm all over the place with what I want and I've never been so confused in my entire life. Last night shocked the hell out of me. I loved it. Every exhilarating second of it—but what does it mean?

Am I ready for more? Do I want something beyond casual sex? The dampness in my panties seems to be screaming, "Yes, you stupid bitch, you do."

I pack up at the end of the day to meet Heather, giving a rueful glance toward Andy's cube. I wonder where he is.

"It sounds like a 'unique' experience to say the least," Heather says, a sparkle of knowledge glowing in her dark eyes. "And, dare I say it sounds like he wants more from you than a one night stand."

I glance down at my hands twisting in my lap. "But that's the problem. I don't know if I want more."

"Why not? Didn't we talk about this the other day? At least giving him a shot takes the 'casual sex' and 'friends with benefits' listings off the table."

My frustration comes out in a huff. "Heather, *you* talked about your damn list the other day, I didn't agree to anything. I like my life the way it is. Uncomplicated and alone. *Alone* doesn't always equate to *lonely,* you know."

"I think thou dost protest too much, my lady." At my deadpan expression, she shakes her head and continues, "What the hell are you really running from, Carla? Have you ever stopped to figure that out?"

Shock sets my skin to tingle. I'm not running from anything, am I? A flash back to last Saturday with my mother snaps into my mind. A sigh escapes and I slump in the chair. "The visit with my mom really sucked the life right out of me. She's such an unhappy person."

"Whoa. Where did that come from?"

"What?" I ask.

"We were talking about you and Andy and then you jump subjects to your mom."

"No, I didn't. You said..." my voice trails off as I see the truth in her words. I did leap from one topic to the next. Damn, I hate how the mind works behind the scenes on crap we don't want to face. Tears form in my eyes and I blink to rid them of the extra moisture. "Ugh. I really hate talking about this shit."

"Yeah, don't we all. What kind of friend would I be if I let you get off the hook that easily? You don't talk about your mom very often. What happened Saturday?"

I shrug, and pick at the food on my plate. "Nothing much. She was her usual judgmental self, putting down what I wear and how I live."

"Ignore her. If I had a rack like yours I'd show it off, too. What else?"

"Really, it was nothing out of the ordinary for her. Next, she launched on her regular man-hater campaign. Ending, of course, with her favorite diatribe on my father."

A look of sorrow crosses my best friend's face, exactly what I'd hoped to avoid and why I don't normally open up about my mother. "I'm so sorry, Carla." She reaches across the table for my hand and I resist the urge to pull away and reject her sympathy. I don't want her pity. I'm not my mom.

I must have mumbled part of that last thought because she says, "Of course you're not your mother—not all men are like your dad, either."

A jolt spikes through my heart and I clench my hand on the table. Heather feels the movement and looks at our joined hands. Is that why I've become content to be alone? Because I secretly fear the man will walk out on me in the end? Unable to voice such raw emotions, I attempt a smile. "Thanks, Heather. I know you're right—but I also know, I don't know what I want."

"The first step is to stop trying to control every interaction and just be yourself for a change."

I nod. I'm too afraid to speak and reveal more than I'd like. And what if I do as Heather suggests and the man still walks out on me? The devastation almost killed my mother. Would I survive such a loss any better?

Movement out of the corner of my eye catches my attention. A familiar pair of shoulders and bright blue shirt slides between people. Is that Andy? He wraps an arm around the torso of the striking brunette at his side. He leans in to place a brief kiss on her cheek, a soft smile curving his mouth.

Blood turns to ice in my veins as I watch the couple walk out. He gives her a big hug and opens the door to her dusty sedan parked in front of the restaurant. He strolls away as my lungs remember how to work and I suck in a sharp breath.

"What's wrong?" Heather asks. "You've got the meanest look on your face."

Cold settles over me as I lock down the growing interest I had in my heart for the rat bastard. Guess what we had was just sex for him. I thought what we shared last night was different. Did he spend the day in her bed when I refused to go back to his place after the bar? Disappoint swells inside and I scrunch it down, refusing to acknowledge the feeling. "Nothing." I force a brittle smile onto my face. "Nothing at all."

By the time I get back to my apartment I'm numb. I can't believe I almost let Heather talk me into thinking this "thing" with Andy could be something more. I never would have pegged the quiet unassuming man as the type to have multiple women on the line, but then again, I also thought he'd be a boring lover, so what the hell do I know?

I can't decide which hurts more, being right or wishing I was wrong.

My phone rings. I glance at the display, it's my mom. "Crap." Today is her actual birthday and I forgot to call. Might as well get the painful conversation over with as soon as possible.

I swipe the unlock on the tiny screen and click answer. “Happy Birthday, Mom.”

“Hmmph. Not so happy when *I* had to call *you*. Did you forget?”

“No, Mom,” I quickly lie. “I was working late and just got home.”

“I heard from your sister.”

“Good,” I try to steer the topic onto something brighter, which in this case is my little sister. “How’s Julie doing? Did you see her this week?”

“No, she’s traveling with work. Said she’d come up this weekend. But she and her rich boyfriend did send me a nice flower arrangement.” She snorts. “Julie never had any taste so I’m guessing the hot-shot property developer picked them out.”

“That’s nice.” Geez, what is with this woman that every nice gesture is turned into something bad with her retelling it?

“Want to place bets on how long their relationship lasts? I’m betting another month, tops.”

“Mom! That’s pretty cold. She’s in love. Can’t you just let it go and be happy for her?”

Another miserable grunt greets me over the line. “Love doesn’t last. You just wait and see.”

The burning pain inside me at seeing Andy with that woman at the restaurant makes me hold my tongue. I want desperately to argue with her, to make her see how negative she's being, but a big part of me fears she's right, so I keep quiet. Thankfully I only have to listen to her for a few more minutes and then we hang up.

Facing Andy at work tomorrow is not going to be easy. Wish I had some dumb stud in bed to distract me. Maybe I'd even call in sick or take a mental health day and go shopping. With inspiration hitting me, I call the guy I went to dinner with last night, *before* I saw Andy. Sure, he might have been a little boring, but he won't break my heart.

"Hey, Brian. It's Carla. Are you free for lunch tomorrow?"

"I've got back to back meetings. How about Monday?"

Resolve hardens my heart as I think of Andy and his other woman. "Sounds great. I'll see you then."

Chapter Ten

Andrew

Carla has alternated all day between avoiding me like the plague and staring at me for minutes on end during two meetings. I swear the woman doesn't know what the hell she wants. She won't talk to me, and according to Outlook, doesn't open my emails unless there are other people CC'd on them.

When she refused coming back to my place Wednesday, I shrugged it off. I could tell by her reaction she'd never had an experience like the one I showed her and I thought perhaps she was still feeling torn on what to do. Should she keep searching for the man with the exciting career who *must* be wild in bed, or take a chance with the guy she only thinks of as a friend? And then I took off on Thursday to see my mom. It's like I came to work to a whole new person.

It's the end of the day and I'm going to push the envelope with her and see how she responds. I need to get some type of reaction from her. "Afternoon, Carla." I lean against her cubicle wall, invading her personal workspace.

The young blonde jolts at her desk and her cheeks turn pink. "Hi."

"What's eating you?"

She harrumphs and returns her focus to the paperwork in front of her. "Nothing. Just busy." Carla's cheeks flame red and I can't tell if she's embarrassed or angry by what happened between us.

"Bullshit," I say.

Her head whips up. "'Bullshit?' What the hell? You don't know me."

Shock tightens my stomach. Yup. She's mad. I lower my voice and lean closer. "Really? I bet I know a part of you no one else in the world knows."

The red of her cheeks joins with the red creeping up her neck, definitely more embarrassed, now. "Leave me alone, Andy. I have no intention of becoming another play thing for you."

"Another play thing? Is that what you think?"

She turns to me, a look of steely determination in her eye. “Yes. Now, leave me the hell alone or I’ll tell your boss you’re flirting with me and I’d like it to stop.”

Heat burns in my chest. “You wouldn’t. That’s total BS. We have the beginnings of something here.”

Ignoring my last comment, she says, “Try me.”

I turn away, deciding to regroup. No way in hell am I letting that parting threat stand. But handling this at work is not the right thing to do, either.

Saturday morning, after a night of drinking alone and resisting the urge to call her, I journey to Carla’s apartment. Unfortunately, she’s not home. If she had returned any of my texts last night I might not have ventured over uninvited, but I couldn’t let whatever distance is building between us to continue. She’ll push me out before I get a second chance to prove myself.

She likes yoga, so maybe she’s getting an early morning workout. I grab a cup of coffee from the bodega across the street, deciding to wait and see if she returns. Luck shines on me within twenty minutes. Carla strolls up the street, dressed in yoga clothes and looking more relaxed than she did yesterday. Good, this might be my only chance.

I wait five minutes and follow, wanting her to catch another elevator before me so she's inside her apartment. I have no desire for a confrontation in the lobby of her building—that could seriously backfire if she's still pissed.

I ring her bell. The sound of footsteps approach the door and I assume she's looking at me through the peephole. Silence ensues. "Carla? I know you're in there. I can hear you. Open up."

Her outraged huff reaches me through the closed door a split second before she opens it. "What do you want? Why the hell are you here?"

She steps back from the door slightly and I take it as an opportunity to let myself in.

"Hey!" she exclaims. "That was rather rude."

I whip around to face her as she closes the door. "And you think the way you treated me at work yesterday was any better?"

"Oh, please." She flounces past me and drops on the couch. "I'm sure you were working your magic on someone else right after." She stares into my eyes, a challenge in her tone. "It's not like what we did really mattered to you."

"I don't know where this crap is coming from. I miss a day at work and you're a different person."

"Yeah, where were you on Thursday? Was some brown-haired woman warming your bed?"

Shock drives me forward to stand in front of her. Anger vibrates through every muscle in my body. "Is that what this is all about? I take a day off and you immediately jump to the wrong conclusion? And where would I have met this mystery woman? In the bar, right after I pleasured you?"

"Did you? How the hell would I know? You probably have a little black book full of women who want to do wild things with you."

My anger dissolves when I see she's more jealous and hurt than truly angry. "Is that what you think?" I lower my voice and step closer. "You think what I shared with you is something I do all the time?"

"I don't know! I don't know *you*. We had one mediocre night together," I wince at her description, "and then you start coming on super strong and sexy. It's nerve wracking!"

I sit in the chair next to the couch, eager to reach out and take her hand, but worry the timing is wrong. "You do know me, Carla. I've never been anyone but me at work or anytime we've talked."

Distrust flashes across her face. "Uh-huh. Sure."

I'll prove to her I'm not some nameless, faceless man she brings home. Six months of working together... she's got to know a little bit about me, right? I refuse to believe she's this selfish, spoiled brat she's pretending to be at the moment. "Where is my favorite place to order lunch?"

She snorts. "Oh that's easy. Every time it's your turn to pick for delivery you go with Ray's Pizza." The humor leaves her face immediately. "That's not really knowing someone."

"Name a movie I saw last month."

She stares off toward her kitchen. "I don't know what in the hell this proves. You saw the latest action flick starring Bruce Willis, half the guys from the office went with you."

"Who organized this year's fantasy football team in the office?"

"Ugh. You did. That was annoying as hell."

"Do I own a car?"

Her face scrunches up. "No, I don't think so."

"What's my favorite color?"

"How in the hell would I know?" Her head whips back toward me. "Give me a break."

I run a hand through my hair, unwilling to give up. "Think, Carla. You're not some unobservant twit. You've chosen to be purposefully blind where I'm concerned, and you should ask yourself why." Her expression starts to shut down and I realize I may have pushed her too hard. "What color do you see me wear the most?"

"Well..." she relaxes into the couch. "I do recall you wear a lot of bright blue ties."

"Bingo. Because it's my favorite color."

Her eyelids drift lower and she fiddles with the tie on her yoga pants, "Yeah, well, it does go great with your eyes."

A huge smile breaks across my face. "See? Was that so hard? You do know a little about me."

She snaps to attention and straightens in her seat. "I still don't know who you were with on Thursday."

"I spent the day with my sister, visiting our mom."

Her face freezes. "You have a sister?"

"Yeah, a twin. Hair and eyes the same color as mine, almost as tall, big pain in the ass..." My voice trails off as I watch the play of emotions cross her face. Understanding seeps in. "Shit, did you see me with her on Thursday night and think she was my date?!?" Horror and humor fill me in equal parts. "Date my sister? No way! Didn't you notice we look alike?"

Mortification flits across her expression. "Uh... now that you mention it, I guess you did look a little alike." I laugh and she cracks a smile. "You could have been one of those good-looking couples who look like a matched set together. Hey! It was an honest mistake."

"So, you think I'm good-looking?"

A crafty look enters her eye. "Nah, it was totally your sister who made you look good."

I laugh, the tension I've held the past day easing out of me. "All this could have been avoided if you'd talked to me."

"About what? We're not an item. We haven't even gone on a date."

Determination fills my soul. "I'd like to change that. Give me another chance." She hesitates and I grab her hand, laying a soft kiss on her fingers while slowly running my thumb across the back of her hand. "You like what I made you feel in the back room of the bar, didn't you?" She nods. "There's a lot more in store for you... if you just give us a chance."

She glances at her watch. "Do I have to answer, right now? I need to shower and be someplace in an hour."

"Is it *Dress for Success*?"

She looks at me sharply. "How did you know?"

"Because I pay attention, Carla. You may pretend to be this prickly woman to keep men at arm's length, but you're not all sharp edges. You have a depth to you. I've seen it."

"Well then, care to put your money where your mouth is? I'm helping to process donated items today. It's my least favorite job and I could use a hand."

Hope swells when I realize this could be the first brick in taking down her emotional wall. "You're on. I'll get us lunch while you shower."

Chapter Eleven

Carla

The warm water cascades over me, easing the last bit of anxiety from my body. I can't believe I thought his sister was another woman he slept with! Thank God I didn't follow my first instinct, which was to storm up to them on the sidewalk and yell at Andy. That would have been humiliating, especially since I'm always the one preaching I don't need a man.

What Andy made me feel on Wednesday... it's not about *need*, it's about *want*. My nipples tighten as I recall how liberating it felt to be blindfolded and pleasured. I want that sensation again. I want to feel more. And that cute little accountant might be just the one to give it to me.

I resist the urge to tweak my hard peaks and the overwhelming desire to pleasure myself in the shower. I hurry through my washing, worried Andy will return with lunch while I'm still in the bathroom. I pick a pair of tight jeans that showcase my ass nicely, and a snug top to display the cleavage revealed by my push-up bra. If I'm thinking more about that man than I want, then damned if I'm not going to drive him to distraction every chance I get.

I put on light make-up and give my short hair a quick blast with the hairdryer. By the time I finish, my phone vibrates.

It's a text from Andy. *On my way up. Can you let me in?*

Yup.

Within five minutes, we're seated at the kitchen island and eating. I'm hyper aware of him sitting next to me, his jean clad thigh brushing against my own. I've caught him stealing a few sly looks down the front of my shirt. Good. That was the goal when I picked it. If I can keep him off balance maybe I can get the upper hand on this puzzling, but attractive, man.

We clean up after the meal and leave for the elevator.

"You've got a nice place, Carla."

"Thanks," I say while hitting the button for the lobby. "You almost sound surprised."

Andy shrugs, his hands in his pockets making the movement look cute. "My sister is a slob. I never know what to expect in a woman's apartment."

I laugh, the idea of Andy turning his nose up at a beautiful woman with a messy apartment strikes me as hysterical. "You're a hard guy to figure out."

"Me? *I'm* hard to figure out?" Andy coughs and it turns into choking.

The elevator opens. "You okay?" His choking stops and he glares at me. "What? You think you're an easy guy to understand?"

"I think *you're* the one who's a hard nut to crack. Not me."

"Me?" I say as we walk across the lobby. "Aren't I the ideal hook-up? I like to have fun with no strings attached. What guy doesn't want that?"

Before I even anticipate Andy might react to my statement, the man pins me against the wall near the front door. "You're more than a hook-up, can't you see that?" His big blues eyes stare into mine, daring me to disagree.

"I—"

His lips descend on mine, covering my mouth with their warmth and intensity. After a moment, the tip of his tongue traces along my bottom lip. His voice comes out soft, the heat of his breath fanning my face. "If you don't expect much from the man you're with, then why waste your time with him?" He kisses me again, this time delving deeper, encouraging my tongue to play with his. "*You* are worth more. Don't ever forget it."

A throat clears, the sound coming from the direction of the elevators. A glance reveals it's the building manager, arms loaded with tools and supplies. "Sorry to interrupt. I need to get by."

Heat rushes to my face and I hear the harping voice of my mother in my head, belittling me for such uncouth behavior. Andy nods to the man as he goes by, unconcerned by being caught. I fan my cheeks after the older man passes.

"Oh, please," Andy says when he sees my actions. "Is my little durian embarrassed by some innocent PDA? Is this the same woman who opened my pants in the elevator a week ago?"

"Durian? What's that?" I refuse to acknowledge my less than stellar drunken behavior of that Friday. We all have low points, and that was mine. Examining *why* it was a low point for me is something I'd like to avoid facing.

"A durian is a prickly fruit." At my look of confusion he continues. "Have you ever seen the greenish brown fruit with spikes all over it in the produce section?" I shake my head. "Well, it's thorny on the outside, but sweet on the inside." He tugs a short lock of my hair before stealing another brief kiss. "Like you."

A smile lights my face and curious warmth spreads in my chest. Sure, he may have just referred to me as a god-awful looking piece of fruit, but it was a sweet comparison, nonetheless. Andy grabs my hand the moment we leave my building, and holds tighter when I try to tug free.

"Would it kill you to hold my hand?" he asks.

His blunt question flusters me and I glance away. "Uh... no." I look back toward him with humor. "Unless you've got some rare skin to skin transferrable disease, but then I would've gotten it when we..." I belatedly realize I'm babbling, so I shut up.

Andy laughs and gives my hand a tug. "Yeah, if I did have something nasty like that, you'd already have it."

Holding his hand feels strangely... intimate. Like we've made a connection in a crowd with the simple physical contact. Warmth travels up my arm and I like it.

A glance at Andy reveals a smug, almost satisfied expression on his face.

"What are you so happy about, mister?"

In a flash, the look is gone, to be replaced by a soft glow of contentment. "Nothing much." He raises our joined hands. "Nice to hold the durian without getting pricked."

"Ha! Keep it up. I can turn the bitchiness on in a heartbeat if you miss it. Just let me know."

We ride the subway, Andy not letting go of my hand the whole time. I felt a little unsure at one point, and tried again to remove my hand from his. He held fast and wouldn't let go. It was oddly comforting. Once we arrive at *Dress for Success* I make a stand.

"Okay. I'm cool with the handholding. It's cute. But not here, all right? I need to get work done and not be tethered to you like a lost child."

Andy's startled laughter spills out and he releases my hand, raising both of his in a surrender gesture. "Relax, Carla. I can find other ways to keep my hands occupied." I walk past him and he lightly smacks my ass as I enter.

I glare back at him and he smiles. "You wore those jeans to tempt me. Don't deny it. I'm just succumbing to what you planned all along."

The afternoon zips by in a blur. Andy charms everyone he comes into contact with, his ready smile and easy-going manner making him popular among the weekend crew. At one point, in the back room, Andy pinned me to the wall for another soul-searching kiss. Damned if that man doesn't have a way with his mouth.

At four o'clock we wrap up and leave. Conflicted feelings battle for supremacy in my mind. Do I trust what I've seen of Andy or brush him off before we take things further? Despite the great day we've had together, I still need time to figure out what's happening between us.

Andy takes my hand again as we exit. "Want to grab dinner? Round out our date nicely with a full stomach?"

I trip over my own feet and catch myself with the help of his steady hold on my hand. "Date?" I don my snarkiest expression. "I thought dates started with dinner?"

He shrugs, unconcerned with my bitch face. "They can start with breakfast, Dury. No rules to what a date has to be."

"Dury? Where did that come from?"

"When you get all distant and standoffish I think of it as your prickly coming out. Dury, durian fruit?" His devilish grin calls me, begging me to smack it off his face. "It's okay though, I'm getting used to it. Think it's your defense mechanism. Bet you do it unconsciously."

Considering I put quite a bit of work into being a bitch, I let him think what he wants. Me, being defensive? I don't think so. Apparently the disbelief shows on my face because Andy stops our trek to the subway, turning me to face him.

"Who hurt you, Carla? Who made you think all men run from a good woman when we find her? Was it that Johnny guy you mentioned the first night we were together?"

Shame fills me over my actions that night. I cannot believe I did such an insensitive thing as to call out another man's name. Half asleep or not, it was a shitty thing to do. And it certainly makes me examine my behavior a little more closely than I'd like.

I duck my head, avoiding his piercing gaze. "Hey, I'm sorry about my thoughtless slip. Johnny was just a college fling. We spent a week together and that was it. Nothing more."

Andy steps closer, pulling our clasped hands up to his chest. "If not him, then who? Who made you think men can't be trusted?"

Unbidden, the image of my father fills my mind. A shudder runs over me and I pull away from Andy's warmth, breaking our clasped hands. "I've got to go. I had fun today. Thanks." I step away, toward the street, raising my hand to flag down an approaching cab.

"Wait!" Andy's voice rises over the traffic noise. "Dammit, Carla! Talk to me!"

The cab veers to a stop in front of me and I slip inside, shaking from the image and feelings Andy stirred up. I know I'm running. I know it's childish. But I can't handle this with him staring at me. I need to be alone.

Do I really not trust men because of my father? Have I always treated each man as a short-term fling because I couldn't do the simplest thing in life and give my trust? My vision blurs as tears gather. What a crappy way to end a nice day.

Chapter Twelve
Andrew

It's Monday and Carla wouldn't answer my texts yesterday except to tell me she was spending the day with Heather. I hope her friend talked some sense into her. Maybe time with her will have put Carla in a better mood. Standoffish, shrewish, and confused is more than I can handle after no communication for the rest of the weekend.

"Morning, Carla." I stop at the entrance to her cubicle, trying hard not to look too interested. "Feel like getting lunch together later?"

"Er... umm. I have plans."

"Really? Sure you're not just avoiding me?"

"Shhh!" she says while looking to see if anyone is listening. "Not at work, Andy!"

Tension seems to coil every muscle in her body and I'm thinking she could do with a little distraction at work. Let that tightness out. "Really?" I run a finger down the cube wall, squelching the desire to touch her creamy skin. "You've been working hard lately, Carla."

"Yeah, well, my dream isn't corporate work forever and I need to pay my dues to build a name."

I lean in over the cubicle wall, lowering my voice, "I never said my dream was corporate work forever, either. You underestimate me."

"No! I didn't mean you... I just need to—"

I interrupt her. "You need to lighten up."

"Lighten up?" The red creeping up her cheeks is not from embarrassment. "Working my ass off is the only way I'll be able to control my life and start my own advertising firm one day."

I thump the fabric wall lightly, eager to get her to meet my eyes. "Giving up control is another way to take control." She's staring down at her desk again, ignoring me. "Who do you have lunch plans with?" I ask on a whim. I think I've got her number.

"Oh? Um... no one you know."

I thought she was lying to blow me off, but maybe I'm wrong. I tilt my head to the side and smile. "Try me."

"The big guy from the bar. Brian." A smug look forms on her pretty face, almost like a challenge. "He's a stockbroker. Did you meet him?"

Bile churns in my stomach. I can't fucking believe after Saturday she's running to another guy. I won't be so easily dismissed. I hold my emotions in check, unwilling to let her see what her admission does to me. "No, but I remember him." Easing away from the steel and fabric partition, I head down to my own little corporate cube. "Have fun."

The idea of Carla and Brian having lunch together haunts me while I pass over a spreadsheet again. My Dury is a complicated woman. Mine? Do I have the right to think that after a one-night stand and a few stolen moments? I know she likes what I'm doing to her—I've never had a woman be so responsive to a few little slaps on the ass.

While I have no hidden desire to become a true dominant or submissive, I did do research online over the weekend about the lifestyle. She definitely fits the classic mold of a controlling woman who needs to let go to enjoy sex. In a submissive role, she'd be trusting her lover to fulfill her every desire. But, I doubt she'll listen to me explain it, especially after she just announced she's having lunch with someone else. I'll have to show her.

As the idea percolates, I smile. This is going to be fun.

At eleven-thirty I mosey down to her desk. "Can you spare five minutes?" My innocent smile firmly in place.

"Huh?" Carla looks up at me, a distracted look on her face.

"Give me five minutes, Carla. I'm not asking for a lot."

Her expression turns suspicious. "What are you up to?"

Walking around the partition I grab her hand and pull her up out of her chair. "Shhh... Just follow me."

"Andy... I'm not interested in playing your games at work. And I need to leave to meet Brian in a little bit."

"Five minutes. That's it. Surely you can spare that for an old friend?"

I lead her into an empty, windowless conference room and lock the door behind us. "When did you make plans with Brian?"

She blushes and looks away. "It was after I thought you were with another woman on Thursday."

"Ah yes, my *sister*. But now that you know that's not the case, why are you still going?"

"I forgot about it and canceling last minute seemed *really* bitchy."

A chuckle escapes me. "You save all your bitchiness for me, is that it?" Slipping a handkerchief out of my pocket, I fold it and press it softly to her lips. "Bite down on this and don't make a sound."

Heat fills her gaze as she allows the gag to slide between her lips. "You can take the gag out anytime you want, Carla. You can tell me to stop if things go too far."

Her eyes widen but she nods her head quick enough. "I'm going to spread you open on this conference table and lick you like you've never experienced before." Lifting her by her hips, I place her bottom on the cool slab. "I bet not even Johnny could do a better job."

A small choking sound comes from her, but I'm not sure if it's laughter or mortification that I've brought up her ex-lover's name again. Hell, I figure if he was worth a damn they'd still be together, so I think teasing her is fun.

Pushing her skirt up around her hips, I see she's prepared for her sexy lunch with Brian. I tamp down my jealousy and admire the beauty before me. I will make her mine. Smooth skin peeks between the tops of thigh high stockings and her silky red underwear. "You think the brokerage guy knows how to tongue a woman right?" I grasp the crimson material and pull her panties down her thighs and over her heels, slipping them into my suit coat pocket.

Spreading her legs, her shaven, glistening folds of skin reveal she's eager and ready for my attention. Even if she won't admit it. "I bet *Brian* is good at getting his dick in and nothing else. Doesn't think of the long game."

Stroking with a feather touch, I brush her exposed folds. Moisture starts to form at her opening, exposing the arousal she'd rather ignore. "You want me, Carla. You want this. Why do you like to hide it?"

Unable to answer around the gag, she shoots me a look of pure evil. God, I love riling her up.

I kneel on the floor and pull Carla to the edge of the table, encouraging her with a small push to lean back and relax on the wood. The musk of her arousal fills my senses, stirring my semi-hard cock to full mast. Planting light kisses on her inner thighs, I nibble every few inches, causing her to jerk on the table. "I bet *I* could make you come without ever touching your clit."

A tremor courses through her as I bend my head to taste her slick flesh. Using both hands to pull away her outer folds, I slowly lick from her core up to the hard nub, pulling away at the last moment before I connect with the sensitive spot. "Hold your legs under your knees." She complies. "That's it... now pull them closer to your chest."

Doing so effectively opens my access to her sex and tight little pucker. "Would you like a good tonguing,

Dury?" I smile to lessen the tease. "There's no prickle to you now. Just sweet acceptance." Without waiting for an answer, I point my moist tip at her pink rosebud and lick. Easing my thumbs down to either side of her bottom, I spread the skin further and work my tongue in deep.

When I press all the way into her ass, my nose touches her wetness. The satin flexibility of my tongue stretches her slowly, igniting all the nerves trapped in the tight ring of muscle.

Carla's hips wiggle, but I have to say, the gag is working nicely and not one order escapes her. Moving up, I burrow my tongue into her pussy again. Long deep strokes, lapping up every drop of sweet, tangy liquid—then, at the end, I drag my tongue to her clit.

The delicious sound of her grunts and murmurs spur me further. Time races by and I don't have much left on the clock. "You want to come?" The whimpers turn high pitched, indicating her agreement. "Did you know it's better sometimes if you wait?" I slip two fingers into her wet passage and pump. Once they are slick I ease one out and tickle her back door, testing her reaction.

A wild squirm tells me it's not painful and I press my middle finger in to the first knuckle. "Waiting can give you an even bigger orgasm than instant gratification." I look up to see if Carla is listening only to see her head tossing side to side in pleasure.

Leaning over her glorious pussy once more, I suck her clit deep between my lips. My two fingers thrust back and forth, the lower one working into her bottom going deeper on each pass. Judging by her increased movement and muffled grunts, I'd say her moment is close.

"God, you taste good." Her back bows off the desk at my words. "That's right, you like hearing me tell you how sexy you are." Carla's hips circle and buck, trying to get my mouth back onto her mound. "Look at you, my worked up sales exec. Who would have thought you'd be squirming here on this conference table looking like a wanton hussy?"

A frustrated grunt comes from behind her gag. Her face lifts from the conference table to glare at me. I slam my fingers into her harder until she lies back once more, lost again in the feel of my hands.

Glancing at my wrist, I see my time is done. I stand between her legs, pulling away from her. Reaching forward, I pull the gag from her mouth. "How was that? Did I get your engine running?" I smile down at her flushed face. "Consider that your second lesson—waiting for release."

"Damn you!" she says, indignation and arousal battling for supremacy in her tone. "You can't stop now. I'm close to coming."

"Shh…" I rub my hands down her legs in a soothing motion. "My five minutes are up."

An angry glint comes into her eye and she reaches between her legs to touch herself. "Fuck you. I'll do it myself."

Grasping both hands in one of my own, I pin them over her head on the table. "You will not."

"What?"

I press my erection against her sensitive mound. "You feel how much I want you?"

"Yes."

"I want nothing morc than to do you here and now."

"Then do it!"

I shake my head, "No, baby. When I take you again we're going to be on a bed and you're going to be begging me to fill you."

"Then be prepared to wait a long time, you prick!" She bumps her hips up, trying to knock me off. "God, I'm so horny. Not cool, Andy. This is borderline cruel."

"I'll make you a deal." I press forward once more, letting my cock rub along her heated core. Her full breasts strain up, begging for me to squeeze them.

"And why would I listen? I'm going to see Brian soon and I bet he'd be happy to get me off."

"You mean he'd try. But I know you. You'll ruin it with shouting orders at him. Never relaxing enough to trust him to please you."

Her breath whooshes out in an angry huff. "How dare you! Get off me this instant or I'll scream."

"The truth hurts sometimes, Carla."

She bucks her hips again and a jolt of fire shoots through my cock.

"Jesus! This is so frustrating! Why can't you just get me off?"

"Like I did the other day?" Her eyes fill with want and she nods her head. "Ah... but what was in it for me?"

"Good God, Andy. Is that what you want, a quick fuck?"

"No," I say while stretching her arms tighter over her head. Leaning down, I nibble along her neck. "I want much more than just a quick fuck."

"But what if I don't?" Her hard nipples show clearly through her bra and blouse.

"Your body betrays you. You want more."

"My body wants to come! You just worked me up and left me hanging."

"Ready to hear my deal?" I say before locking my mouth behind her ear in a kiss.

"Fine."

"Don't fool around with Brian and wait for me."

"You? Why? So you can tease me again?"

"This is just the beginning." I whisper in her ear, and her body betrays her once again with a hard shiver. "I plan on teasing you for hours. Bringing you over and over again."

"Deal."

Chapter Thirteen

Carla

We unlock the conference room door, glancing up and down the hall before leaving. “Hey, are you going to give me my underwear back?” I ask.

“No.”

I stop dead in my tracks, “Excuse me?”

Andy shoots me a crooked grin and saunters down the carpet. “You’ll be more aware of yourself without them on. Trust me.”

Yeah, and I’ll be horny, too. Jackass. And this guy thinks he knows what he’s doing? Sending me off all sexed up to be with another guy?

Staring at Andy's tight ass as he walks away only makes me think of grinding my heels into his backside to pull his hips deep between my thighs. Damn him! Why can't he just accept I don't want to be with an accountant? *Maybe because you aren't so sure anymore.* Talking about numbers when I get home from work is not my idea of stimulating conversation.

A twinge in the back of my mind whispers a future with Andy could be something else, but I quickly lock it back up and ignore it. I detour to the ladies room to check my hair and makeup—good thing, too. Andy's cotton gag smeared my lipstick. As I dab to correct the color, my sex throbs in time to my heartbeat.

A shiver runs down my spine recalling Andy's heated mouth locked onto me just a few moments ago. His soulful blue eyes bored into mine when I tried to glare him into doing my bidding. Is he just a better lover than the guys I've been with lately, or is it something more?

The slick wetness from my arousal is quite distracting, and I realize I'm going to have to clean up before I meet with Brian. I wonder if he could smell it. Maybe I should ignore Andy's deal and get the pounding I want from Brian. Who the hell is Andy to tell me what, or whom, to do?

I enter a bathroom stall, twisting the knob to secure the metal door. Grabbing a handful of toilet paper, I reach between my legs to dry myself off. The roughness of the commercial paper rasps against my engorged clit, sending a staccato beat of want coursing through my veins. Reaching a finger between my swollen folds, I tickle the raised flesh. A soft moan escapes me as a door swings open a few feet away, followed by footsteps and two of my co-worker's voices. Dammit!

Pushing my skirt in place, I toss the tissue in the toilet and leave the stall. Maybe I'll seduce Brian at lunch. I'm not sure I want to wait for Andy.

"And then I say 'Sell it now, take the two hundred thousand gain and walk away.'"

I smile at Brian's retelling of a mid-morning work conquest. We're seated in chairs opposite each other—the tiny bistro had no booths available, and thus my secret desire to persuade him to fondle me under the table during lunch was thwarted.

"Good for you," I say, in what I hope is an interested and enthusiastic tone. "I bet your boss is thrilled."

He shrugs, flashing me a good ole boy grin. "You're only the favorite until the next big deal closes. Comes with the territory."

His broad chest pulls against his pressed shirt, straining the buttons. He's obviously been working out and getting bigger, even if he's late on catching up his wardrobe. He looks good, but the desire I felt when I first met him is absent.

I don't want Brian's flesh pressed against mine just because I'm horny. If I'm honest, the flesh I want is Andy's. Am I letting him worm his way into my heart?

My arousal abated during the boring lunch conversation, thank God, but Andy was right. I'm much more aware of my privates with no underwear on. No one here knows of my secret dirty-girl behavior with my prim suit skirt covering the evidence.

A glance at my watch indicates we've only been here for thirty minutes or so. I don't like that I'm thinking only of Andy and not other men. It's very unlike me. Maybe I can prove to myself it doesn't have to be Andy. That any man will do. I raise my eyebrows at Brian. "Want to find a closet somewhere and have some fun?"

Brian chokes on his water, sputtering before regaining the ability to speak. "Here? At the restaurant?" He glances around at the packed space and cranes his neck to look down the bathroom hall. My arousal perks back up at the idea of being taken in a public building. "I'm not so sure that's a good idea."

My heart sinks, along with my burgeoning desire. I thought this guy was exciting with his big muscles, strong air, and blatant good looks. But he's acting boring, like all the others.

All the others before Andy, you mean.

Heather's advice from yesterday screams to the forefront of my mind, "Give the guy a chance. He's making a real effort to get to know you. I don't think he's like the other men you've dated."

I lean in to whisper, hoping to bring Brian around and block out my inconvenient conscience, "I'll let you take me hard and fast from behind. You can bend me over a crate of napkins in the storage room."

Brian fumbles with his silverware and it clatters to the table beside his plate. "Um... I think it sounds wild," his low voice ensures only I hear his response, "don't get me wrong. But I need privacy to really 'get into' the moment. All these people and the noises would freak me out."

I sit back, dismissing the moment, and him, in my thoughts. "Fine. Maybe another time."

Sensing my change of attitude he rushes forward, "How about later tonight? Back at your place?"

My thoughts return to Andy and the "deal" we made. Damned if just the thought of that man in my bed doesn't get my motor running. "Sorry, I have plans."

His disappointment shows clearly in his expression as he signals the waitress for our check. We end the lunch with some chitchat and small talk, but all of a sudden he doesn't seem as sexy as I'd hoped.

We enter the parking lot and he pins me to the outside wall of the restaurant, perhaps in a last ditch effort to show me he can be spontaneous. His mouth grinds hard against mine, the chicken he had for lunch lingering on his tongue. My first instinct is to push him away. He's not the man I really want. But dammit, I don't *want* it to be Andy, either!

Clumsy hands grab my breasts and squeeze. Last week I would have been grinding up against his crotch, eager to continue. But now, I just want to get out of here.

A couple rounds the corner and Brian steps back like he's been burned. "Sorry, Carla." He smiles awkwardly at the pair before returning his attention to me. "Want to try the back seat of my car?"

Would Andy be apologizing to me right now or would he have picked a better spot before trying to rile me up?

Holy crap, here I am comparing other men to *Andy*. What is my life coming to? “Don’t worry about it, Brian. I need to get back to work.”

And just like that, I walk away from him, determined to not waste more time on a guy who doesn’t appeal to me and worries too much what other people think.

Back at the office, I walk slowly down the aisle to my desk. Andy locks eyes with me and a feral grin seeps over his expression. How can he possibly know I didn’t mess around with Brian? I settle in my cubical as my phone twerps, a glance reveals a new text message from Andy.

How was lunch?

I rise up in my seat to see if he’s staring at me over the other desks. He’s not.

Fine.

Gee, you don’t look like it was fine. You still look on edge.

Pressing my thighs together under the desk, I try to think of a witty rejoinder. Immediately the image of Andy’s head between my thighs flashes across my mind. Without warning, my desire ratchets to where it was when I walked out of the conference room. An arousing pulse beats in a growing circle from my crotch. Just the thought of seeing what Andy has in store for me is driving me crazy. God, I feel like I’m in college again.

Work is no place for what I'm feeling. I decide to lie to the responsible party. *No, I'm fine.*

Is your pussy still wet for me?

His naughty words on my phone are unexpected and they trigger a jolt of adrenaline. Could he be interested in doing more, right here, right now, at work? Suddenly my teasing of Brian at the restaurant seems small and insignificant. *No.*

I bet you want to touch yourself right now.

Of course I didn't a moment ago, but now all I want is to pull my skirt up, scoot my ass to the edge of the chair, and rub myself 'til I moan.

I type back, *No.*

Rich masculine laughter sounds from a dozen feet away. *Sure, you keep telling yourself that. I'll see you after work.*

Heat flames my cheeks as I slam the phone into a desk drawer, shutting it with enough force to rattle the frame. Deciding I can't let this man dictate my pleasure any longer, I stalk to the ladies room. Time to take matters into my own hands.

Out of the corner of my eye, I see Andy rise from his desk to follow me. Damn him! I'll find peace in the only sanctuary in the office off limits to men. I quicken my pace, eager to get into a stall and bring myself some relief.

I know my release will be a good one and hopefully it will clear my head enough to focus on work and not *him*.

The door whooshes closed behind me and the wetness pooling at my opening begins to slick the top of my thighs. God, I'd love a big dick in me right now, pumping and thrusting while I go over the edge. Two ladies stand at the sinks, washing up. I shoot them a strained smile, hoping they leave soon.

I wait for them to exit and check the other stalls. No one is here, I should be able to let loose. The door sounds behind me and I whip around to see who else has come in. Freakin' hell, it's Andy!

"You shouldn't be in here," my voice hisses out. He turns the deadbolt on the door and faces me.

"I knew you couldn't wait," he says while stalking closer. "But I'll make it better for you." He slips his tie from around his neck and takes out his familiar folded handkerchief.

My eyes widen as I contemplate why he might want to use his necktie.

"You're going to be loud," he says with a wicked smile. "Put this in your mouth and do as I say."

The folded cotton square slips between my lips again and Andy fastens the silk tie behind my head, securing the material in place with a gentle tug. The gag feels naughty, but not scary.

Andy leans in, whispering, “Do exactly as I tell you. Trust me, it will be worth it.”

He presses against my shoulders slightly, encouraging me to walk backward and place my back to the cold tile wall. Leaning in, he nibbles my neck, planting heated kisses in a wet path to my cleavage. Excitement sings through me. God, how could I ever have thought Andy wasn’t stimulating?

“Lift your skirt,” he says. I rush to comply. The cool wall sparks a tingle against my bottom, making me very aware of everything going on and exactly where I am.

“Spread your legs.” Andy steps back and leans against the metal frame of a bathroom stall while I do as instructed. “Good.” His erection presses against the front of his tailored pants. One hand rests at his waist and I watch eagerly to see if he plans to open his pants.

“Touch yourself, nice and slow.”

My fingers ease between my thoroughly aroused flesh while the gag muffles my small sigh. I circle the hard nub with a feather touch, which brings me close to the edge rather quick.

"That's it, Carla. I see how ready and swollen you are. I'd like nothing more than to get on my knees and bring you with my tongue."

I nod enthusiastically, but he shakes his head, never taking his eyes off my fast moving fingers. It's such a turn on to watch him devour my every movement.

"Stick them inside and pump."

I whimper, but do as he says. The slick walls clasp my fingers tight and a small squishing noise reaches my ears. First one finger, then a second, plunge in a relentless pace.

The metal scrape of Andy's zipper ricochets around the empty bathroom. He pulls out his erection and strokes it while I follow his last command. One fist wraps around his length and I can't rip my eyes from the sight of him pleasuring himself.

"You do that well," he says on a ragged breath. "Use your other hand to work your clit. Nice and slow. I'll tell you when to speed up."

Some inner part of me wants to rebel at his words, but the physical gag works to silence my personal turmoil as well, allowing me to let go and do as he bids. The moment I touch the tiny spot, electricity shoots into my body. My legs feel rubbery and start to shake.

"Slide down the wall. Sit on the floor and spread your legs."

The chilly tile, the stifling gag, and the awareness we're in the ladies bathroom combine to push me higher. I feel the release just out of reach and pump my fingers faster to drive myself over.

"Not yet, slow down," Andy says, pushing himself off the frame and walking toward me. The musk from his aroused naked flesh coats the air as he brings his cock a few inches from my face. Pre-come glistens from the tiny slit and I long to take the smooth head into my mouth.

His fist starts to work slower, like he's struggling to contain his own sensations. "Pinch your clit."

The rubbing feels so good I'm not sure I want to stop. At my hesitation, Andy reaches a hand out to grab my hair under the knotted tie, tilting my head back at an angle, forcing me away from the tile wall. "Do it, baby."

I pinch the flesh, as ordered, and a small shudder hurls through me. Andy steps to my left, straddling one of my splayed legs, and stops caressing himself.

"That's it," he encourages as I continue to pump two fingers and squeeze my clit once more. His grip on my hair shifts, tilting my face up, forcing me to gaze at his cock and distant face while I pleasure myself. Passion etches his features as his erection pulses slowly in the air.

"You're ready, Carla. Rub it hard and fast."

I do as he bids, my body arching off the tile, a muffled scream making its way past my gag. Andy holds me firmly in place while the first wave of release washes over me, its intensity nothing I've ever felt on my own. A hot hand latches over the gag in my mouth, locking away even more of my sounds.

"More," he coaxes softly, "you're not done yet."

I writhe and buck on the cold tile floor, pumping myself as hard as I can while the currents of pleasure continue to pulse even higher. The fingers pressing into my cheeks and the hand grasping my hair somehow increase the height of my release. Behind the white cotton and silk tie, my moans pour out one after the other, muffled and contained.

A door opens inside me and a rush of emotion spills out with my orgasm. Tears leak from the corner of my eyes and trail down to the silk tie. No experience in my life can compare to this moment. Stars explode in my vision and I close my eyes to enjoy each wave of energy wracking my frame.

"You're stunning when you finally let go."

As the shivers lessen and the aftershocks slow to nothing, I notice the grip on my hair is gone and Andy has pulled his hand from my mouth. I open my eyes to see him stuffing his erection behind his fly, wincing as the zipper shuts it away.

He unknots his tie and removes the handkerchief. My voice comes out dry as he lifts me from the floor, smoothing my skirt over my hips with his free hand. “But you didn’t come,” I say.

Andy places a tender kiss to my mouth, dipping his tongue in and sending a fire back through my blood. “This was for you. My time will come later tonight. That is... if you’re willing.”

No longer desiring to hold Andy at arm’s length, I’m willing to see what else he has up his sleeve. “I look forward to it. How about my place at seven?”

“Yes. It’s a date. A real date, Carla. I plan to take you to dinner first.”

Chapter Fourteen

Andrew

My second chance stands on the other side of Carla's apartment door. As I pace the length of the hallway carpet, doubt rages through my mind. I never expected things to progress this well based on our one-night stand almost two weeks ago. Granted, she's been willful by making a lunch date with the brawny stockbroker, but the accepted dinner invite tonight proves my recent attentions have been worth the effort.

She was receptive to the blindfold and the gag, and even allowed me to control her peak. But how much further do I push her? My cock stirs in my pants at the thought of tying her up and having my way with her.

Maybe, with the help of the gift I've brought, we'll try the blindfold idea again and I'll get her on her knees.

The hallway around me loses focus as the blood rushes to my prick. I want more than anything to thrust into her all night while she calls out my name. My labored breathing echoes in the hall, indicating I'm too keyed up to be aiming for seduction. Waiting will make the orgasm stronger, but picturing my gorgeous co-worker writhing around her fingers on the bathroom floor isn't an image I can shake easily.

Running my hands through my hair, I make a quick decision. If I can't get tonight right, I might blow my last chance with her. And based on what I'm seeing from her more and more, I think she's worth the effort. With a grim expression, I look around and proceed to the stairwell at the end of the hall. Stale air, with a hint of concrete, wraps around me as the fire door closes.

I stand perfectly still; listening for any sounds to indicate I may not be the only one in the stairwell. I place the small gift bag on the floor at my feet. Grabbing the white cotton fabric from my pocket, the one I'd folded earlier and shoved into Carla's mouth, triggers an answering lurch in my cock. Damn that was hot. Hurrying to free myself, I unzip and take my erection in a firm grasp.

Wrapping around the girth, I twist and pump halfway down, caressing the sensitive head at the end of each stroke. Thoughts of the beautiful blonde spread open on the conference table invade my mind while my mouth waters at her remembered sweet, tangy taste.

Teasing and playing with the gorgeous young woman all damn day has left my body tight as a wire and eager to explode. My eyes drift down as I stroke myself, the rhythm picking up as I recall how she reacted when I tongued her ass.

God, she's so responsive—she's fucking hot to watch. The way her head tilted back while I fisted her hair in the bathroom, the burning look in her eyes when my cock bobbed inches from her nose. All too soon the moment is upon me and I cover the slick head with the handkerchief.

My peak rushes forward, sending quivers racing through me. My balls pull up to my body and streams of come jet from the tip, to be caught in the cotton. A sigh escapes as tension seeps from my muscles. Shoving the used handkerchief in my pocket and my semi-hard dick back in my pants, I grab the gift bag and proceed back into the hall. I'm sure I'll now be able to perform much better this evening when it really counts.

Determination and confidence pours through me as I knock on her apartment door. I plan on giving her the night of her life. She's bound to see we're right for each other when I leave her more satisfied than any other man has before.

Carla answers and ushers me in with a charming smile. "Nice to see you're on time."

I return her smile, "It's never good to keep a lady waiting."

"Huh," she quirks an eyebrow, "you had no trouble making me wait today when it suited you."

I take her arm and pull her into a light embrace. Running my hands up and down the soft silk of her tiny black dress, lingering on her curvy ass, I whisper into her ear, "That's not the same kind of waiting."

She pulls away and moves toward the small galley kitchen. "Green looks good on you, Andy."

Glancing down at my vee neck sweater and slacks, I shrug. "Clothes are clothes. I don't think about it much, but thanks. Your dress looks hot, but you know that or you wouldn't have picked it."

She laughs, running a hand over her curvy hips. "Thanks. Glad you like it. I know the dress looks good, but it's still nice to hear." Her eyes dart to the small bag dangling in my hand. "Is that for me?"

"Yes," I reply, setting the package on her coffee table. "It's for later, after dinner."

"You gonna make me wait to open it?"

I grin and nod. "Haven't we already determined it's better when you wait?"

She grabs a previously opened wine bottle off the counter, one hand reaching for the stopper at the top. "Whatever, Andy. I'll do what you say... for now." A heated look crosses her face. "Where are we going for dinner?" The pop from a cork fills the air between us and the gurgle of pouring liquid follows. "Do you like white?"

"Yes."

Carla sashays closer with two glasses, working her curves for all she's got.

"Thanks," I say while taking the glass and leaning in to give her a kiss.

Our mouths touch and I detect a hint of mint toothpaste. With my free hand, I cup her head, tilting her to grant better access. Our tongues dance for a bit and my semi-hard state soon becomes a thing of the past.

The full raging boner doesn't reflect the recent quickie I gave myself in the stairwell, but if I hadn't done it, I'd be coming in my pants.

She sets her glass down on the table. One warm hand traces the muscles in my chest while the other reaches for the one between my legs. "Someone is certainly happy to see me."

I stare deep into her eyes. "How could you ever doubt that?" Uncomfortable by the clear emotions in my gaze, she ducks her head and looks away. "Do you know what you want in a man, Carla?"

She pats my cock, sending jolts of anticipation through me. "I know what I want right now."

This isn't going quite how I'd like. I need to dig a little deeper before I give her what she thinks she wants. I move her hand from my crotch and raise her fingers to my mouth to nibble on them, "And you'll get it… in due time."

"Why all the games, Andy?" she says, pulling her hand from my lips.

Confusion tinges my voice, "Games? Isn't that what you're doing?"

A spark of annoyance crosses her features. "You're the one dictating to me, so how is it I'm playing games?"

This wasn't how I pictured starting our evening, but I guess I'd better lay things on the line. I take a drink of wine to fortify myself then set the glass on the kitchen table next to hers.

"You come on to me in the cab, we have sloppy sex in your bed, and then you pass out. I try to revive you with my hand and you dream of an old fling, calling out his name." She burns in remembrance and turns away, arms wrapping around her middle. "You call our night together tolerable and then sporadically return my texts." She grabs her glass, props a hip against the counter and takes a long swig of wine. "Then you pick up another guy the next week, spend time with me on the weekend, and then see *him* again on a lunch date." She's not looking at me now, but staring off in the direction of the stove. "I think I'm right in saying you're the one playing games, lady."

"Oh, yeah? What about you?" She tears her gaze from the stove to stare at me. "Pulling me into the storage room at the bar?" Anger colors her tone. "Playing with me in the conference room until I could barely see straight? Gagging me and having me masturbate on the bathroom floor?"

I step toward her, leaning close to pin her to the counter top. "And you loved every damn second of it."

Her face sears under her conflicting emotions. "I've never felt this way, Andy. It confuses me."

Placing an arm on both sides, I trap her in place. "Why are you so scared, Carla?"

"Because I can't control it!" And there it is, her biggest fear just slipped past her careful wall of indifference.

"Sex isn't about control, at least not how you're thinking."

"How do you know what I'm thinking?" she says with a slight sneer.

Ignoring her poke of nastiness, I grab her face in my hands and hold her still while I kiss her hard. By the time I let go, both of us are breathing fast. "Because I've been where you are."

"Oh, really? And where would that be Mr. Perfect Accountant?"

Recognizing her jabs for what they really are now, a way to cover her fear, I let it go. "You're lost," I say, then plant a kiss on her forehead. "And I plan to show you the way."

A snort escapes her, but that's better than her earlier anger. "How?"

I kiss the end of her nose, striving for light-hearted and silly. "How about we have dinner first?"

She smiles, relaxing in my arms. "Okay, dinner first. Do you like Italian?"

"Love 'em." I wiggle my eyebrows, "The women are especially passionate."

"You're incorrigible!" She's laughing and the moment of difficulty is behind us.

"All joking aside, I'd planned dinner for us at the piano bar up on Christopher Street. They've got a great menu and the atmosphere is nice."

"Sounds good to me."

We leave and in minutes we're walking on the sidewalk, hand in hand. I like the feel of her grasp in my own. It's warm and reassuring, like we're a good fit, despite what she'd like to believe. Her constant prickly attitude is a defensive mechanism, and now that I've got her figured out in that regard, I refuse to let her sharp words get to me.

A warm spring breeze blows in our faces, bringing with it the smells of the city plus the hint of warmer days to come. Sadness skirts over me as I remember the springtimes of my youth, camping trips and hanging with Andrea and our folks. Maybe I'll be able to create similar memories in my future with the person I start a family with.

"Do you like to camp?" The question blurts out impulsively.

Carla tilts her head, glancing at me while we walk. "We went on a couple of trips when I was younger, when my dad was still around."

"Did your parents divorce?"

She pulls away slightly, forcing me to tighten my grip to hold her hand. "Um...no. Not exactly. He left us when I was fourteen."

I stop dead in my tracks, turning the tiny blonde to face me. Her father leaving their family makes perfect sense. The worst of her emotional walls were brought on by that single act. "I'm so sorry. That had to be incredibly hard on your family."

Carla shrugs, unwilling to meet my eyes. "You don't need to be sorry. It wasn't your fault. He just up and left one day."

"No note? No phone calls? What did your mom think?"

A short sound of laughter erupts from her. "My mom? She put on a brave front for the first few weeks. When the cops couldn't even trace his car they suggested it might have been deliberate on his part." Her voice turns soft, a trace of bitterness creeping into her tone. "Like he took on a whole new identity to start over. Apparently it's not uncommon."

I pull her toward me, wrapping my arms around her in a hug. "That's awful, Carla." Her stiff body hesitates in my embrace for a moment and then relaxes a fraction. I cup a hand over the back of her head and hold her close, determined to ease her old pain. I had asked who hurt her so badly, but I had no idea it was her own father. How the hell does a guy battle against a past like that?

Resolve settles inside me. I'm not going to give up just because she's got baggage no one should have to suffer through. Her past has made her who she is, just like mine has for me. She pulls away from my embrace, awkwardly glancing up the sidewalk.

"That's the place on the corner, isn't it?"

I nod and tuck her hand in the crook of my arm, determined to have her closer to my side for the rest of the walk. "Not all men are like your father."

She glances up at me through a fringe of bangs. "I'm starting to realize that."

In a few moments we're at the restaurant, the maitre d' smiling when he sees me. "Ace! Good to see you. I saw the reservation and hoped it was you." I reach a hand out in greeting and the older man ignores it, drawing me into a quick hug. "We've missed you!" He pulls back and wiggles his eyebrows suggestively at Carla. "Is this the lovely lady who's taking up so much of your time? Will you be coming back soon?"

"Good to see you, Gino." I place a hand in the small of Carla's back. "This is Carla, we work together."

"Work?" His expressive eyebrows shoot up again, making his aging forehead a mass of lines and wrinkles. "You are working somewhere else?"

I shake my head, hoping to cut him off before he says any more. “We’ll talk later, Gino, okay? I don’t want to keep the lady waiting.”

“Yes, yes.” He waves a hand toward the main room of the restaurant. “Excuse my manners. I’ve got a table waiting for you close to the floor. Just in case you change your mind.”

Carla smiles at the older gentleman, but I can tell by the look she shot me that she’s wondering what’s going on. Gino leads us into a dark interior. There are small lamps lit at each round table, and a huge piano dominating the center of the restaurant with a small dance floor in front of it.

We sit down and Carla says, “Who’s Ace?”

Chapter Fifteen

Carla

Andy glances behind me with longing. A look over my shoulder reveals he's staring at the piano. Interesting. I wonder what is going on. I cock an eyebrow at him, waiting for him to answer.

"I'm Ace. It's a nickname I picked up while playing."

"Playing what?"

He gestures with his chin to the glossy black instrument sitting under a spotlight. "I played the piano professionally before I came to work at the advertising agency."

A tingle of shock races through me. "Get out. You're teasing me."

"No really, I did. I told you I didn't dream of corporate life forever."

"Well, yeah, you did, but I assumed you meant you'd like your own accounting firm one day or something."

He shakes his head, a small melancholy smile on his face. "You know what they say about assuming."

"Come on! How could I have ever guessed you were a musician? Why did you stop playing?"

Andy settles back in his chair, looking like he's getting comfortable to tell a tale. A waiter comes over with a big smile and an open bottle of wine.

"Ace! Gino told me you were here. Good to see you." He pours us two glasses of red and then places the bottle on the table. "Michael said you were on the schedule for this weekend. It's a treat to see you here during the week, my friend—especially since it's been so long!" At my look of askance at the wine he says, "Forgive my presumption. This is Ace's favorite and I grabbed a bottle when I heard he was here. Do you mind? It's a house red, good body."

I reach for the wine, eager to hear more from Andy when the waiter leaves. "Thank you, sir. I'm sure it will be terrific."

The dark haired gentleman smiles my direction. "She's a cute one, Ace." He bobs his head at Andy. "Be sure to keep her a little while."

Andy's eyes heat with desire. "I'll do my best to keep her happy, Glenn, trust me."

Glenn nods his approval and leaves to attend other diners.

"Well?" I prompt. "Going to keep me hanging?"

Andy takes a sip of his wine, staring into the glass, a hint of sadness in his eyes. "No, that wasn't my intention. It's a difficult topic and I'd hoped we'd have a light evening."

"Difficult, huh?" I smile to show I'm teasing. "Did you knock up a waitress?" Andy grins and it encourages me to keep going. "Cause a scene over an affair with a married woman?" He chokes at that one and puts his glass down. "Oh, I know–burn down the kitchen when you had a threesome with the waitress and the midget washing dishes?"

Laughter erupts and the sad look I saw in his eyes leaves. "You really think I'm the type to have an affair with a married woman?"

I shrug a shoulder and reach for my own glass. "Dunno. You might not have known she was married... would explain how you know so much...," I fidget in my seat, uncomfortable with how to phrase his sexual expertise, "stuff."

His eyes shine with barely contained mirth. "Are you trying to find out why I stopped playing piano or why I'm such a creative lover?"

My cheeks burn at his bold question. "Can't blame me for being curious, right? I mean, how does an accountant learn all the things you've tried on me?" I take a drink and place my wine back on the table.

"Well..." His voice trails off and he leans in closer. "We've already established I'm not just an accountant. Maybe I learned things in my days working night clubs."

"Maybe..." I pick up my menu, excited to be here, eager to draw out our easy speech as long as I can. I hadn't expected to feel this relaxed with Andy, or this intrigued to learn more about him. He's like an enigma, wrapped in a puzzle, masquerading as a simple man. All this time I worked side by side with someone I dismissed as boring due to his job. Really shows how superficial and petty I'd become.

Why this man would go to so much trouble when I've been nothing but a difficult bitch is beyond me. Does he expect me to become his sex slave or something? The thought brings on a mental squirm, indicating I'm not entirely adverse to the idea—especially if I'd get to feel like I did today after he completely controlled my pleasure in the restroom.

Andy's eagle eye gaze narrows on me. "What are you thinking about, Carla?"

"Why me?" I blurt out before I can stop myself. "Why did you pursue me when all I've ever been is self-centered and bossy to you?"

Andy's face softens and he reaches for my hand, forcing me to put down my menu. "You're too hard on yourself. You've been more to me than that, and more to others around you, too."

I look away, not sure I'm comfortable with his observations, especially when it seems like he's not really answering my question. "Uh-huh."

He tugs my hand, bringing my attention back to our joined fingers. "When your friend called you last month, panicking about her phone? You talked her off the edge, gave her guidance. I heard you." I raise an eyebrow at him —he's grasping at straws. "Don't look at me like I'm full of shit. I'm not. That's just one thing. How about when the office manager, Judy, was out sick for a few weeks over the winter? You took her dinner several times and even babysat her kids when she went to the doctor."

My eyes widen. "How did you know that?"

"I pay attention Carla. I've watched you—not in a creepy stalker kind of way, just as a man interested in finding a good woman. I've seen you rush out to yoga class and still stop to give the homeless guy on the corner money for soup. Three weeks ago, I saw the flyer for *Dress for Success* that you slipped into every woman's cubicle before they arrived at work." He pulls my fingers to his mouth, placing a kiss on their tips. "You may act like an unfeeling, prickly shrew around the men you invite into your life, but that's not who you really are inside."

Tears fill my eyes and I jerk my hand to pull it away. He holds fast, staring at me like he's looking into my soul, seeing me like no man ever has.

"You have a good heart, Carla. And that's what I want in my life." He smiles to lessen the intensity of the moment. "And besides, anyone else wouldn't have challenged me mentally."

"Really?" I say, a touch of smarm in my voice. "'Cause you're such a genius you haven't found an equal?"

He gazes at me with a superior air of serenity in his expression. "The best things in life require hard work. If you gain something easily you don't value it as much."

Glenn bustles back to our table, a tray in one hand. "Gino told Beverly you were here, too. She sent out several appetizers for you to nibble on." He sets down a long platter holding at least half a dozen different artfully arranged delicacies.

"It looks scrumptious." I beam up at the server. "I didn't see this on the menu."

Glenn waves a hand, dismissing the generous gesture. "Sometimes she tries new things and wants to share them with her friends. Please, eat. Ace is like family."

Andy smiles his thanks and picks up a square of toast with tomatoes and spices on it as Glenn leaves.

"They seem to love you. When did you stop playing here?" I reach for a seasoned shrimp on a stick.

He finishes his appetizer before answering, "I didn't technically stop, just lowered my appearances to once every other month or so." He gazes longingly at the grand piano once more. "I can't give it up completely."

Maybe now is a good time to push for more from him. "Why did you cut back so much?"

He eats another appetizer before responding, his expression more relaxed than when we first mentioned the topic. "I wasn't earning enough to pay my mother's medical bills, so I took a better-paying job I got my degree in."

I want to ask about his mom, but I stick to a safer topic, hoping he'll tell me when he feels like it. "You went to college for accounting?"

Andy forks a shrimp and nods. "My parents wanted to make sure I had an education to fall back on if music didn't pay the bills."

Surprise fills me at the easygoing way he describes his parent's subtle direction of his choices in life. "Wow. They sound... supportive. And far-seeing."

A touch of sadness fills his eyes again, but not for himself, I have a feeling it's for me. "That's what most parents are like. Not all of them are like your dad, taking off and leaving those he's responsible for." His face twists into a bitter mask. "I'm sorry to say it, Carla. But your father sounded like a coward."

A part of me rages inside to defend the man, like I did for years with my mother when she spewed her hateful words. But this time, I settle the conflicting emotions inside me and nod. How long am I expected to deny the truth? A good man stands by the people he cares about, he doesn't leave when the going gets tough.

"Where's your dad?" I ask. "Why isn't he helping with your mom's bills?"

"My dad died a few years ago. Unfortunately, he was ill for a long time and everything they had was eaten up to pay for his ongoing care. My sister doesn't make a lot with her freelance writing, and that's *with* her degree in journalism. When my mom got cancer two years ago we tried everything. But there's only so much Medicare will cover."

"Medicare? How old is your mom?"

"Seventy-eight. Our folks had us late in life. She was forty-four when we were born and my dad was fifty-two." His face takes on a warm glow, as if recalling a fond memory. "We had a great life growing up. Having retired parents was kind of nice. They made time for *all* our school functions, had money to spare for long trips—Dad even coached my little league for a while."

Warmth washes over me as I realize all that he had... and all that my sister and I missed. "That sounds nice. You're very lucky."

"I know. And watching them—how they felt about each other showing in small ways— helped me figure out what I wanted in life. Which reminds me," he pushes back his sweater sleeve to check the time. "Do you mind if I call my mom before our meal arrives?"

"No. Not at all." Andy takes out his cell. "Would you like some privacy?"

He shakes his head. "She's in a coma and is mostly unresponsive." My heart clutches at his words, delivered so matter-of-factly. "We said our goodbyes when she was still aware, but I'd like to think hearing me play might make her more comfortable and feel loved."

Shock settles over me when I comprehend exactly how strong this seemingly unpretentious man is. Would I have the same healthy outlook if it were my mother lying in a coma? The inner voice I'd like to ignore chimes in with, *Probably not. You have too much anger where she is concerned.*

Andy signals for our waiter and we place our dinner orders, under the heavy guidance of the attentive man's suggestions. Right before he leaves, Andy says, "I'd like to play a song, Glenn. If that's alright?"

Glenn's face splits into a huge grin. "It's more than alright, Andy. You go right ahead."

Andy nods his thanks and hits the dial button on his phone. "Hi Iris, it's me. How's she doing?" After a slight pause while the person on the other end answers. "Thanks. Would you mind holding the phone for her?" He rises from the table and holds the phone out to me while gesturing to the piano. "Would you hold it while I play?"

"I'd be happy to." Our fingers brush when he passes it to me, electricity tingling up my hand.

Andy leans down and plants a soft kiss on my lips. Pulling back slightly, he stares into my eyes. "This one was one of my mom's favorites, but I chose it for both of you."

My heart starts to trip in my chest and I'm speechless, unsure what to say or do in the face of this man's confidence and heart-melting attention. As he walks to the piano I take a deep breath. I think I nodded my understanding to his statement, but my insides are feeling so knotted with anticipation I may have sat there like a lump, staring.

He settles on the black bench and turns on the microphone sitting on top of the piano. Holy crap, he's going to sing, too. The moment the mic clicks on and the speakers kick in, all heads turn in his direction. I clutch the phone in my hand, eyes locked on the man sitting in the small spotlight.

"Good evening, everyone. Management has graciously allowed me to play a song for you tonight." He looks over toward the doorway we came in and nods. "Your normally scheduled player for the evening will be on at nine. Is that correct, Gino?"

"That's right, Ace." The maitre'd calls out. "Thank you."

I glance behind me and see a collection of employees gathered near the entrance, some from the kitchen, too.

Without warm up, Andy launches directly into a song, his fingers dancing across the keys with no effort. The strains of a familiar tune reach me, as Andy's eyes lock onto mine across the distance.

The opening words of *She's Always a Woman to Me* wrap around me, transporting me into the Billy Joel song with the spell he's weaving.

The beauty of his voice, pitched perfectly, creates the sensation like the entire restaurant has disappeared and it's only he and I in this moment. As he hums between stanzas his gaze drifts from me to the keys and back again, closing the distance between us with an almost magical air.

Words to a song I know by heart take on new meaning as I listen to every phrase, and apply them to myself. He's singing about an independent woman, like me, who makes no excuses for her behavior and often appears harsher than intended.

The last line of the chorus about a woman changing her mind stabs at me, jarring me with its truth.

I can change my mind about how I look at men and relationships without giving in. I can still be me and allow someone into my life. He's so gorgeous, sitting there, singing his heart out. Tears moisten my eyes and blur my vision as the poignancy of the moment breaks through the hardened shell I've erected around my feelings. I can't believe this man I've ignored for months is the sweetest, kindest soul I've ever met. How does he know me better than I know myself?

Tears trickle down my cheeks when he sings about a woman being kind and then cruel.

I muffle a sob as I clutch the phone.

He finishes with humming and sustaining the last notes, lingering over the keys. He bends his head as it ends, breaking our eye contact. The restaurant erupts into applause and the energy flowing through the room crashes into me with a sensation of acute awareness. Aware of the beauty, aware of the sadness, aware of the depth in this man... this man I'm seeing for the first time.

Andy casually stands, comfortable with the attention, and executes a short bow. He returns to the table as I stiffly wipe the tears from my face. He slips the phone from my grasp, says goodbye and thanks the person on the other end again before disconnecting the call. Andy pockets the device, then reaches for my hands, pulling me to stand.

"You may be a prickly fruit, but I like you just as you are."

I leap at him, no regard for how I look or that we're in public, plastering myself to his front as I latch my mouth over his in a deep and steamy kiss.

Chapter Sixteen

Andrew

"Dinner was absolutely magical, Andy. I've never had a night like that in my entire life."

Her admission brings a surge of pride. "Thanks, I'm glad you enjoyed it." I give her hand a slight squeeze while we walk back to her place. "I was a little worried when I saw the tears. But the tongue jammed down my throat set me straight soon enough."

Carla's laughter rings into the cooling evening air. "Yeah, you didn't seem too concerned at the time."

"All kidding aside, I feel like tonight was our first 'real' night together. The first night with no pretenses, no jockeying for power or control or hiding ourselves. Just two people getting to know each other."

"More like one person finally getting her head out of her ass..." Carla's voice trails off, with a slight trace of bitterness directed at herself.

"Hey now, enough of that." I quicken my pace when I see the awning to her building. "You still have a present in your apartment yet to open."

Carla pauses on the street corner, titling her head up to me in the harsh illumination of the street lamp. "You mean you don't plan on romantically kissing me at my doorstep to leave me dreaming of your awesomeness all night long?"

I reach down, wrapping her in my arms and pressing a kiss to her smiling mouth. Our lips meet and she sighs, parting her mouth to allow me entrance. Our tongues dance as our passion rises and heat swirls through me. I reluctantly break off our embrace. "Does that feel like the kiss of a man who's willing to end the night before it really starts?"

"Hell no. It feels like the kiss of a man I'd like in my bed all night."

My heartbeat quickens at her implied offer. "Really? Not going to boot me out the moment you're satisfied?"

She shakes her head and continues our journey back to her place. "Call me crazy, but a man romantic enough to sing to a woman in a restaurant earns a whole night to prove his sexual prowess."

I smile into the darkness as I envision her reaction over the blindfold, silk ties, and small finger vibe I have waiting for her in the gift bag. It's going to be a fun night.

"That sounds fair to me."

"Holy cow." Carla's face splits into a huge grin. "You bought me a Vanilla Bondage Kit and a tiny vibrator? How does this little thing work?"

I laugh as I take the package from her and tear it open. "It's designed to slip onto the end of a finger, to assist with extra stimulation." I demonstrate its two positions. "You can rotate the vibrator under your finger tip to use against your sensitive skin," I wiggle my eyebrows as I glance down at the juncture between her thighs. "Or you can twist it to behind your finger, so it adds to your *personal* ministrations."

Carla pulls her black dress over her head and launches it toward the foot of her bed. "I think you've got to be the coolest guy ever."

I smile at her eagerness and pick up the creamy satin blindfold. "Ready to try this?"

"As long as I get to watch you undress first."

"Deal."

I toe-off my shoes and race to add my clothes to the growing pile, excitement fueling my movements in my haste to explore and entice the curvy blond. She laughs as I whip off my sweater, then she comes closer to smooth my hair down.

"What do you have in mind?" she asks, running her fingers down my neck.

"If I told you it wouldn't be a surprise."

Openness and acceptance shines in her expression. She nods once, steps back and reaches for the blindfold. She slips the mask over her eyes. "I can't see a damn thing." Carla tugs it into place. "Although, it does smell nice."

"That's the vanilla scent. Did you think the whole Vanilla Bondage Kit was just vanilla-colored satin goodies? I think it's a nice touch. And hey, not to be obvious, but not-seeing through a blindfold is the whole point," I say. "It can be freeing." I step closer, already turned on by her willingness to try new things without questioning me to death. Leaning in, I nibble one delicate earlobe. "Wasn't it freeing in the dark when I smacked your bare bottom and you squirmed against my hand?"

"Yes—but I don't get why."

“Don’t over analyze it, Carla. Just accept it. You think too much.” I slide the small finger vibe onto the index finger of her right hand, and then press the button on the back to turn it on. “How does that feel?”

“Nice. Kind of odd. What am I going to do with it?”

“You’re going to touch yourself with it.” I press her shoulders to lower her to her knees.

“Uh-huh. And why am I getting to my knees while you’re still standing?”

In answer I push the black boxer briefs down my hips. My cock springs free into the cooler air of the apartment. A sigh escapes me at the thrill of what’s to come. “So you can reach my cock easily.”

“What—?”

The slight opening of her mouth to speak is all I need. I nudge the head of my prick past her lips and silence fills the bedroom. Cradling her head with both hands, I grip loosely behind her ears, lacing my fingers. “That’s it, work the head in nice and slow.”

Her suction increases as she starts to bob on my cock. “I’m going to guide you a bit and use some pressure. I want you to pinch my ass hard if it gets too much for you.” She nods around my cock, canoeing her tongue on the underside of my shaft.

God, she's a natural. Once I get her brain turned off, she falls quickly into the submissive role. Which means, with her penchant for wanting control, she'll eventually be excellent playing the top as well.

Rocking my hips forward slowly, I'm careful not to press too hard. She'll need to limber her jaw to get me in deep. Moist heat engulfs the top half of my shaft as she wraps one hand around the base of my cock to guide it in. Unlacing my fingers behind her head, I dig the tips into the base of her skull, where it meets her neck.

Slowly I massage the tense muscles there while coaxing her head a little deeper on my cock, "That's it, baby. Relax and take it all in."

She's a little past the halfway point, but I feel her body responding to my voice and the tension easing from her. "Nice. Now put that finger vibe where you need it."

She touches herself with the new toy and a slight moan vibrates over my flesh in her mouth.

"My God, you're so sexy sucking on me." Her red lips ring my erection and I can't pry my eyes away from watching the length slide between them. "If you could see how fucking hot you look you'd be impressed."

I still my hips, despite how good it feels, and allow her to control the depth, every now and then exerting a little pressure behind her head to keep her trying for deeper. The hand holding the base of my shaft starts to pump in time to her mouth.

"I bet that sweet little pussy of yours is getting wet with all your hard work." Thinking about her touching herself prompts me to move my hips again, eager to increase the pace and depth of her attentions.

The sensations pouring through me indicate I've only got a few minutes before I'm past the point of no return. I plan to make the most of them. Gripping behind the vanilla blindfold, I hold her head still. "Don't move for a moment, baby. Let me see you play with yourself."

Pumping forward with my hips a mere inch and then back, I watch the vibrator-sheathed finger work her clit. The heat and wetness surrounding my shaft feel exquisite, and I'd love to come when she does, but I'm saving the ending for being deep inside her.

Her fingers twirl faster on her aroused clit as her body twitches. I pull my hips away, not wanting her to bite down on me when she comes. She tongues the swollen purple tip in frantic stokes, trying once or twice to shove back down on my length, but my hold on the back of her head restrains her.

Soon, her sounds of release fill the air—whimpers, groans and low guttural keening bounce off the walls of her dimly lit bedroom. I shake with my own need, the satisfaction of seeing her come in such a glorious fashion sending a warm glow through me.

Reaching under her arms, I pull her from her kneeling position. I remove the blindfold and see tears leaking from her shut lids.

A fist of guilt grips my heart, "Carla? Are you okay, honey? Did I hurt you?"

She snuggles up against my bare chest, my cock still slick from her attentions poking her stomach. "No, you didn't hurt me. I just didn't expect the rush of emotions. My God, that was intense."

Running my hands over her tousled hair, I try to soothe her jittery feelings. "I know what you mean. Losing control so completely is sure to unlock lots of things we'd rather not examine in the light of day."

She leans away to glance up at my face, "When do *you* lose control? It seems like I've been the one with all the lessons so far."

Cupping her cheeks, I kiss her mouth, allowing my need and desire to shine. My voice comes out rough and low, with my emotions hanging for her to hear, "It's all about giving and taking. I give the control to you sometimes, and sometimes you give it to me. That's what love and trust is."

"We walk on the wild side a little bit, together?" She reaches down and strokes my aching erection.

"Yes." A sharp intake of breath fills the air between us and my hips lunge of their own accord, into her firm grasp. "Would you like to try tying me up?"

Her smooth hand grips my cock harder at the mention. "You mean I get to do what I want to you for a change?" Her eyes hold a glint of mischief in them and I only hope I can hold back my release long enough for her to enjoy herself.

"Hey, the kit came with vanilla satin ties. I'm game if you are."

"Oh my God," she shivers. "I think I'm getting close again just thinking about it. Climb onto the bed, mister, while I grab the ties."

Chapter Seventeen

Carla

The sense of power flooding my blood as I knot the cream silk around Andy's wrist feels quite heady. I can do what I want, when I want... as long as he doesn't say no.

"You're getting off on this aren't you?" he asks.

A short laugh sounds in the bedroom, "Whatever gave you that idea?" The grin stretching my skin feels maniacal.

"Maybe the passionate expression, maybe the glint in your eye, maybe the energy vibrating through you..." he trails off and settles against the pillows propped under his head. "You look eager."

I straddle his hips and lean forward to kiss him. "Because I am." Our mouths lock for a few minutes and his pulsating cock twitches against my ass. "Want me to blindfold you?"

"I'd rather watch if you don't mind. You're sexy as hell."

Warmth burns in the pit of my stomach at the hungry look in his eyes. He's managed to rile me up damn good and show me more in the last few days than I've discovered in twenty-eight, almost twenty-nine, years of living. I never would have expected his mild-mannered exterior in business clothes to contain so much raw passion.

Every direction he's given, every slight show of strength, every upper-handed situation he's engineered… a shiver cascades over me when I think of what he's done to me and made me do.

"I like you watching me," I whisper.

"You do, huh?" He nips my bottom lip and tugs it into his mouth for a moment. "And why is that?'

I reach behind and grab his erection. A sharp intake of breath reveals he's more turned on than his casual attitude expresses. "You make me feel beautiful when you do. Like everything I do turns you on."

He thrusts his hips, bumping the swollen head of his cock between the cheeks of my ass. "Everything you do *does* turn me on."

Perhaps that's what's been lacking in my previous encounters with men. I knew they wanted to fuck me, but I never knew if they wanted *me*. To know Andy has seen me at work when I'm cranky, bitchy, stressed out and crazy—and still wants me—feels exhilarating and potent.

"You feel pretty randy, Andy."

"God, I've been dying to get back inside you."

"How long do you think you can last?"

"I'm embarrassed to admit it, but not long. You sucking my cock and getting off just about made me lose it."

The forceful thrust of his length pumping toward my throat, and his gentle pressure behind my head flipped my switches more than I anticipated. To be lost in the moment and trust he'd not push too far and choke me drove me higher than a kite.

"Let's slow you down and then I'll build you back up, okay?"

A ripple down his torso tickles the inside of my thighs, "You're the boss. Whatever you say."

I move between his legs to lick and kiss his thighs. Ignoring his stiff prick, I focus on the hairless tender spots on his inner, upper thighs, rubbed clean of hair from friction during exercise. A nibble on the soft skin sends a jolt of reaction through him and emboldens me to try more.

Taking his shaved sack into my mouth, I tease one slinky globe with my tongue and reach between his clenched butt cheeks. “Relax, Andy. Let me in to play.”

“It feels so good, I can’t help but tense up.”

Kneading his balls in one hand, I encourage him to lift his left leg and bend his knee, putting one foot flat on the bed. “That’s it, I can reach your tight little ass now.” A glance up reveals he’s paying attention to my every move. The satin ties are held taut in his fists and he’s pulling the material tight from the sturdy bed frame.

The muscles in his arms and chest strain with his effort to remain still. Slipping one finger in my mouth I get it good and wet, licking it suggestively as I pull it out. Andy watches me with a burning intensity and we lock eyes when I reach down to tickle the tan pucker of his bottom.

Pushing past the ring of muscle, I gradually ease my finger in and curve up to the walnut sized gland of his prostate. In my other hand, I hold his sensitive sack, tugging it away from his body as I stroke inside.

His head tosses on the pillow and his body lurches toward the ceiling. “Christ, that’s good.” Andy’s hips come off the bed, angling a bit to drive my finger deeper.

"You like this, don't you?" I say while slipping a second wet digit in.

His breath spills out in a ragged whoosh of air. "Of course. How in the hell do you think I know what it feels like for you?"

"You ever been with a guy?"

A strangled laugh leaves him as I pump steadily. "Oh, God. Slow down." I change my pace and stare at the incredibly sexy man writhing around my fingers. "Liking my ass played with doesn't mean I'm gay. I do it myself sometimes when I jerk off."

The image of him stroking his cock while touching himself like that sends a wave of want coursing through me. "I bet that's sexy as hell to watch." I tickle the sensitive spot inside and his lower back arches off the bed once more. "Do you ever use a toy?"

He grunts in response and tosses his head to the side, checking the restraints. "I need these off soon."

He didn't answer my question. He must be getting really close. "Oh? Do you now?"

Leaning down, I capture his purple head between my lips, licking off the salty pre-come gathered in the slit. I hum in appreciation for the flavor and the vibrations spiral up into Andy. Dropping his balls, I wrap a fist around his base and squeeze tight hoping to slow down his reaction.

Fingering his bottom makes me feel incredible. I never realized how sexy it could be. The thought of using a toy and burying it deep inside him exhilarates me. My own arousal ratchets up at the steamy images and I squirm on the bed.

"I can't take much more, Carla," his voice sounds harsh and ragged.

Sheer power pours through me. I did this. I brought this sexy man to the edge. The bobbing of my head increases and I can't decide if I want to bring him off and swallow or untie him so he can bury himself inside me.

Andy lifts off the pillows, straining the bonds fastened to the headboard. "Please! Untie me!" A choked sob comes out and my pulse skyrockets. Man, he's hot. "I need to fuck you, baby."

Slipping my fingers out of his tight little bottom, I climb up his body, pushing him back onto the bed. "I'll let you loose." An evil grin spreads across my face. "After you lick me for a bit."

Hunger burns across his fierce expression and he nods in agreement. I straddle his head, lowering myself to his mouth. Reaching out with both hands, I weave my fingers through his near the top of the headboard, the ties holding fast under the added weight.

His hot, pointed tongue touches my engorged clit and I jolt, a loud moan escaping me. My hips rotate in a slow rhythm, grinding against his clever mouth.

"God," I rasp into the quiet bedroom. "I think I love your tongue."

A muffled chuckle spills out and I ignore it, driving myself higher from his ministrations. Realizing I'm close, I rise, dislodging my lover from his feast. I fumble in my haste to remove the satin ties, clumsy in my excitement. "By the way, I've got the implant. I won't get pregnant. And I've always used condoms in the past."

"Me, too." He whispers, face glistening from my arousal. "Condoms I mean." His eyes search mine. "Are you sure? You want to take this step?"

I nod, so excited to be with him I don't trust myself to speak.

"Good, 'cause I'm going to do you 'til you scream." One knot comes undone and Andy wraps an arm around my waist. He leans in and captures one hardened nipple, tonguing it and then biting softly.

Moans pierce the air as I struggle with the last restraint. His movements when I played with him tightened the bonds, making the material difficult to loosen.

"Done!" I shout as the last knot slips free.

Quick as a wink, Andy flips me on my back and positions himself at my entrance. "There won't be much finesse. I'm too damn close."

Seeing the look on his face, the masculine beauty of his desire causes a hitch in my breath and a need I don't recognize bubbles in my heart. He slams his hips forward, seating himself fully on the first stroke.

My lower back arches and I push my hips to meet each thrust. Faster and faster he plunges, stretching my walls and filling me. Animal grunts spill from him as he lowers his weight to his elbows, bracketing my body with his size and mass.

Andy nibbles at my ear. "Come with me, baby." He reaches down, grabs my wrists and pins them to the bed next to my head. The heat of his body sears into me and the slight strength he exerts on holding me down sends a thrill through my body.

Each drive of his cock sends me one step closer to the edge. The primal force and keening sounds of desire undo me completely. Screams flood from deep in my throat, echoing back to combine with his guttural moans. "Andy! Oh God, Andy!"

Hearing his name pushes him to his own release and he pistons into me with renewed vigor. The hands at my wrists grip me tighter, pushing me deeper into the mattress. The muscles inside me clasp his length as each pulse of my orgasm rocks through me. Andy throws his head back and moans loudly into the night.

My vision blackens as my own peak continues to ride and I lock my mouth onto Andy's in desperation. We kiss like we're trying to climb into the other's skin and a part of me is shocked by my own reactions. Little by little, the pulses ease and I notice Andy's thrusts are slower.

"Holy shit," he says while nuzzling my neck. "I don't think I've ever come like that before."

Sometime during that spectacular ending he released my arms. I move shaky limbs to embrace him. Sweat mists along the heated skin of his broad back and for a moment I revel in the sheer strength he contains.

"Ditto here."

Andy reaches a hand out to grab a blanket and pulls it across us. The weight of him on me isn't crushing; it's soothing, like he's wrapped around me, protecting me from the world.

My lover shifts to the side, robbing me of the safe feelings and his warmth. "I don't want to squish you," he mumbles while pulling me close.

“You weren’t,” I answer, nestling into the spot near his shoulder, eager to recapture what he’s brought out in me.

“I have a lot I want to say,” he stifles a yawn. “But it can wait ’til later.”

Acceptance and emotion cradle my heart, just as his warm palm cradles my shoulder.

“Good. I’m looking forward to it.”

Chapter Eighteen

Andrew

In the middle of the night I awake, the warmth of Carla snuggled against me, her head under my chin. I breathe in the lingering scent of her shampoo, a light floral aroma. My breath rustles the bangs near her forehead and a soft mew of contentment spills from her.

It feels like a dream come true to finally have her in my arms. All the months of carefully waiting for her to notice me and the contrived questions about accounts so we could talk... all of it led to this night. And if I could change a thing, I wouldn't.

If we had experienced a good night of sex that first time together she probably would have shifted me into some type of fuck-buddy role and I never would have ventured past her emotional walls. I run a hand over her smooth back, reveling in the satiny feel of her skin. A smile spreads across my face in the darkness—no sign of her prickly defenses now.

The intensity of my release and temporary loss of control from last night comes back to me, stirring my cock to life. Damn, that was hot. She's a passionate woman when she lets herself be in the moment. I tilt my face to her forehead and place a kiss against her bangs, wondering if I can stealthily wake her up...

I cough, clearing my throat loudly. She stirs and comes partly awake, probably unused to having someone stay the night.

"Oh, did I wake you?" I whisper into the dark, careful to keep my tone neutral and not hopeful.

Her hot hand trails over my chest and down to my stomach. "I had the most amazing dream. And look at that, you're still here." Her fingers skate below my waist and brush my growing erection. "Oh, and what a nice perk. Looks like all your parts are awake." I can hear the smile in her words as her warm breath fans my chest.

Her hand locks over my arousal and I suck in a breath. "I'm thirty-four, not sixty-four. I'm good for more than one round per night."

She lifts her head and plants a soft kiss on my mouth, her hand teasing me to full height. "Good to know, old man."

Before we lose all track of sense, a niggling worry in the back of my mind has me reaching out to place a hand over hers. "Last night was incredible. Please don't tell me it was another one-off type of thing."

Faint light from the street spills in, slightly illuminating her unsure features hovering inches above my own. "I'm not saying no, but I need time to decide how far I want this to go, okay?"

I let go of her hand and reach up to cup a full breast. "That's better than a no any day of the week."

The peace and calm of our sexually-satisfied sleep is rudely broken by an incessant knocking at Carla's front door. She snuggles in deeper as I glance at the clock. It's only a few minutes after seven a.m.

The banging becomes louder as I nudge Carla. "Someone's at the door."

She mumbles, "Probably just a delivery. Can you get it?"

Warmth swells inside me at the casual inclusion she's offered into her life. I kiss her bare shoulder and reply, "No problem."

I grab my pants and shirt, not bothering with underwear in my haste. The firm knocking continues after a brief respite and I call out, "Coming!"

Carla pushes her bangs off her face and yawns. Her voice carries to me as I exit the bedroom, "I might as well get up, too. We've got work in two hours."

I open her apartment door and my blood freezes. This is no deliveryman. The guy in the hall is wearing a jacket and slacks, a button down shirt and a tie. He looks about my age, but a bit more haggard. His hard visage makes more sense when he opens his wallet and flashes a shiny gold badge. "Is there a problem, officer?"

"*Detective* Donovan. Does a Carla Johnson live here?"

"Yes." I motion behind me. "She's waking up now."

"I need to speak to her. May I come in?"

Unsure if shutting the door on him to check with Carla is a wise move, I gesture with my arm for him to come inside. "Please, have a seat. I'll tell Carla you're here." I close the door after he enters, and face the detective. "Can you tell me what this is about?"

"Are you family?" I shake my head. "Sorry, I can't."

Dread fills my stomach as I walk to Carla's bedroom. She's sitting up in bed with a robe on, a confused smile on her face. "Did you just let someone into my living room?"

"It's the police, Carla. I'm not sure what he wants."

Her face scrunches up in confusion. "I haven't done anything wrong. Maybe it's an issue with one of the neighbors?" She smiles warmly at me, "Although, if something happened last night I can honestly say I didn't hear a thing."

"Why don't you get some clothes on?" I run a hand through my short hair. "I think talking with a stranger in a robe might be a little uncomfortable."

She sighs and moves to her closet. "You're probably right. Wonder what in the heck it could be about. Hope no one's place was broken into. The building has always been safe in the past." In a moment she's dressed in yoga pants and a t-shirt and I stand to the side to let her pass.

"Aren't you coming with me?" Hope shines in her eyes.

Tension from a held breath eases out. "If you want me to, yes."

We pass through the narrow hall to greet the early morning visitor. The officer rises and extends his hand. "Are you Carla Johnson?"

"Yes, I am." She shakes his hand briefly, then settles on the couch and pats the cushion next to her, indicating I should join her. "Would you like some coffee? You caught us before the pot was made."

The tired-looking officer smiles, but it doesn't reach his hazel eyes. "Thank you, I'm fine." He reaches into his coat to withdraw some papers. "Did your mother, Erin Johnson, file a missing person's report fifteen years ago for one David Henry Johnson?"

Carla straightens in her seat. "Wait. You're here for something about my father? Not like a break-in in the building or something?"

The detective nods, his dark hair neat and his expression solemn. "Yes, that's right. I'm here about a development in his case. You put your name in as a person to contact seven years ago, correct?"

Carla's face drains of color as she nods. I reach out across the couch and clasp her hand. "Our family moved out of the city a few years after my dad went missing. When I moved back into the area I contacted the department my mother originally filed the report with, just in case anything came up." She swallows loudly. "Oh my God. What's happened? Just spit it out."

"I'm sorry, Ms. Johnson," he says. "Your father's body was discovered in a deep ravine, during excavation for expanding a road."

She clutches my hand. "Did you just say 'his body'?"

"Yes, ma'am. The coroner's report states he died about the same time frame he was reported missing."

Her voice comes out shaky, "Did the report say how he died?"

"He suffered a severe head wound but whether he died from the injury or exposure to the elements is uncertain at this time. He had no wallet on him or anything of value. His identity was discovered through dental records collected with the original case. It's speculated he may have been the victim of a carjacking and robbery gone wrong. I'm terribly sorry, ma'am."

Carla stares straight ahead while the detective opens his notebook.

"You were fourteen when he was reported missing?"

She doesn't say anything. I scoot closer and wrap an arm around her, squeezing her shoulder to bring her back to the here and now.

"Um...What?" She shakes her head. "I'm sorry. Yes, I was fourteen."

"Do you recall if your father had any enemies or what kind of people he socialized with?"

Carla's face takes on a far-away expression. "Enemies? He got along with everyone as far as I could tell. I think he was in sales. I know he traveled with work sometimes. It was so long ago, I don't really remember friends, outside of people who came to parties."

"Anyone ever seem to have a beef with him or maybe he owed them money?"

"Not that I know of."

"Did your parents fight often?"

Carla's face crumbles. "Why are you asking these questions? Didn't you just say it looked like a carjacking and a robbery?"

"Yes, it *looked* like that's what it could be. But that doesn't mean we don't try and find out exactly what happened that night."

The detective and Carla talk for a few more minutes before he departs, leaving her with his business card. He needs to speak with her mother and is giving Carla a chance to break the news to her first. Carla will need to head out soon. The shock of his visit leaves both of us quiet. Striving for some semblance of normalcy, I venture into the kitchen to make coffee. It takes me a few minutes to find everything and get it going. Carla doesn't get up to help and I'm inclined to leave her to collect her thoughts.

Very soon I've got a hot cup ready and hand it to Carla who's still sitting on the couch, frozen in place.

She takes a small sip of the fresh brew, her eyes meeting mine. "I don't know what the hell I should be doing right now. This feels surreal."

I take a seat next to her and wrap my free arm around her hunched shoulders. "I think you'll need to call in to work and then arrange transportation to her house."

A shudder runs through her frame. "You're right. I'll call into work. There's no way I can tell her this over the phone. I'll have to drive up." Her hand shakes as she sets her coffee down. "I don't even have a car. I'll have to rent one."

Immediately I think of my sister's car. "I can call Andrea and see if she can lend me hers. Do you want me to go with you or would you prefer to go alone?"

She turns to me, her dark blue eyes looking lost and empty. "Thank you for the offer, but I think this is something I need to do by myself. My mom..." her voice trails off. She takes a deep breath and tries again. "My mom can be difficult and I have a feeling she isn't going to take this well."

Chapter Nineteen

Carla

Pounding spring rain pours down as I drive a rented sedan through the dreary morning to my mom's. The roads are slick and the traffic crawls. What would normally be a ninety-minute drive is already taking over two hours.

My cell rings on the passenger seat. One glance reveals it's Andy calling. I click answer and immediately switch the phone to speaker option, setting it on the console between the seats.

"Hi Andy."

"Hey. Are you at your mom's yet?"

"Almost there. The rain has slowed everyone down." Apprehension swirls in my middle, the rhythmic beat of the steady wipers doing nothing to calm me. “I’m so not looking forward to this.”

“I don’t blame you.” A sigh echoes over the phone. “I’m sorry about the things I said about your dad last night. I had no right.”

His thoughtfulness helps to stem the twisting in my gut. “Not your fault. I was right there thinking the worst of him myself.” I stop at a light close to my mom’s house, wondering how I’m going to break the news to her. “Of course, that was because we all thought he’d left. God, what a mess.”

The light turns green and I make a left into her housing development. She bought one of the smaller townhouses two years after I graduated college when she only had Julie visiting sporadically on weekends.

“I feel awful you’re dealing with this on your own. Are you going to be okay on the trip back alone? I could come up if you need a driver.”

I smile, despite the awfulness of the day. “Thank you for the offer. I’ll be fine.” I’ve finally found a guy I want to spend more than one night with and I can’t believe I’m pushing him away. But it’s important to me that I handle this family business alone. I need to clear the air with my mom on a lot of emotional baggage and have waited too long to do so. Would I really want a new lover hearing all our dirty laundry?

"Okay, as long as you're sure. Call me when you're heading home. The weather is bad and you know how New York drivers are." I hear a touch of humor in his last words, as if he's trying to lighten the situation a little. What an amazing guy. And to think I almost missed him due to my own issues.

I use my left turn indicator when her street approaches, driving slower than normal due to the rain. "Alright, I will."

We say our goodbyes and hang up, seconds before I turn into an empty space in front of her place. The pale cream siding looks drab in the grey light of late morning. A lamp from an upper story illuminates the small front bedroom overlooking the parking area.

I didn't call ahead, worried it would start an avalanche of questions I was unprepared to answer. My mom works from home, telecommuting for a medical billing company. I know she's there, where the light is, working in the bedroom she uses as an office.

I take a deep breath and pull the hood up on my light raincoat. Waiting won't make it any easier, so without further contemplation I grab my purse and race into the rain, then up her steps to the front door.

Apprehension fills me once again as I ring the bell and wait for her to answer. God, maybe I should have asked the cop to come. Would that have been easier or harder?

Depends on how you look at it. Easier because you wouldn't have had to be the one to tell her.

No. This might be hard, but it's the right thing to do.

After a few minutes my mom opens the door, her face creasing in surprise when she sees it's me.

"Carla! Come in, come in." She steps to the side and ushers me with one arm out of the rain. "I didn't know you were coming." Her eyebrows creep up her lined forehead. "Did you call and I missed the message?"

I shake my head no and remove my coat. She takes the dripping garment, her eyes traveling over my casual jeans and t-shirt without comment, and quickly hangs the raincoat in the attached garage so the water can fall off in there. When she turns back to me, worry creases her brow.

"Are you okay, dear? It's not like you to drive here unannounced—especially on a work day." Comprehension blossoms across her face. "Oh my God—did you get fired? I'm so sorry, honey."

"No mom, nothing like that. Can we go sit down and talk?"

"Sure." She heads down the entry hall to the kitchen, the small living room opening up to my right as I follow her. "Would you like some coffee? I can put on a fresh pot."

The coffee I had this morning went down like acid, bubbling and churning during the first half of my drive. "No, thanks."

"I'm going to nuke mine. Want to talk at the table?"

Not sure where a good place would be to drop this ball of news, I agree, "Yeah. That's fine."

My voice sounds wooden to my own ears. Perhaps it's the shock of knowing what I know, I'm not certain. One thing is for sure, I'm not looking forward to the next few minutes.

I take a seat and patiently wait while she heats up her coffee, adding a bit more milk to the mug before joining me.

"Well, you've got my attention," she says with a small smile. "What's up?" Her face lights with shock. "You're not pregnant, are you?"

"Mom!" Indignation flashes over my face. So typical of her to think the worst of me. "No, I'm not pregnant. It's nothing about me." My eyes dart away from her, to the large window overlooking the woods behind her townhouse, then back when I muster the courage to speak. "I had an early morning visitor."

She sips from her mug, nodding that she's following me.

"It was a police detective."

Her face loses all color and her body stiffens. "Did something happen to your sister? Is she okay? Is she at a hospital? Why didn't you call me?"

My hands come up in a reassuring gesture, meant to stem that flow of thought. "It wasn't about Julie." She sags a little in her chair, the instant tension gone. "It was about Dad."

She purses her lips, tilting her head to the side in question. "What about your father? A detective you say?"

I nod. God, this is harder than I thought.

She takes another sip of coffee, looking a little flustered but not like she's going to flip out, more like she's trying to work through the *why*. "Was it a development in the missing person's case I filed long ago?"

"Kind of." I look away again, my gut clenching.

"Carla honey, just spit it out."

"He's dead, Mom. They found his body while excavating to expand a road."

She sets her mug down with a heavy clunk. "What happened to him?" Her face hardens as she tries to control her emotions. "Did he die in a car wreck—maybe while living his new life with someone else?"

I shake my head and reach across the table to grab her hand. "No, Mom. The coroner thinks he might have died very close to the time he was reported missing."

Her mouth drops open and she pulls her hand back from mine to cover her mouth. Guilt races across her face, the emotion unmistakable, before disappearing under the red of anger. "That's impossible. The investigating officer told me he thought David left us, that he'd seen it happen time and time again to families in..." She stops mid-thought, but I caught the slip.

" 'Families in' what, Mom? What were you about to say?"

"There must be some mistake. It's not David." She bolts up and stalks from the table, turning when she reaches the counter and leans back against it, arms wrapped around her middle.

I stay seated and watch her carefully. Why was she looking guilty a moment ago? Could she have had something to do with his disappearance? The moment the traitorous thought arrives I squelch it. My mother might be a bitch at times, but she'd never have killed my father. It doesn't add up to her behavior in the past fifteen years.

"It's not a mistake. The coroner confirmed it was Dad by dental records with the original missing person's file."

"No! It can't be right! He's out there somewhere, I know it! He just..."

"Abandoned us high and dry fifteen years ago?" I stand, my own anger getting the better of me. "Why is that option more appealing to you? Does that sound like the man you married? The man who had two children with you?"

"Yes! I mean, no. But the officer was so sure he'd left. I believed him."

"Did you, Mom? Or did you want to? You looked guilty a moment ago." Her eyes widen and she averts her attention to the floor. "What is it you haven't told me all these years?" I step closer, my proximity forcing her to meet my gaze. "What are you leaving out that made you so readily accept the man you'd known for so long would up and desert his family?"

She says nothing, her mouth a thin line.

"Answer me!"

My mother flinches and then crumbles, her shoulders sagging forward. Her voice comes out soft and broken. "We fought that night—about money, bills, you name it.

He packed a bag and took off, saying he was going to visit a client and would do his best to dig us out of the financial mess our lives had become." Tears trail down her checks. "The weather was bad, like today–slick roads and a downpour. I yelled at him and practically chased him out of the house, furious with our situation."

I reach out and touch her shoulder. "Why didn't you tell me any of that? Couples fight all the time. It's normal, especially when times are bad."

"Because the officer looked at me as if it were my fault. Like I'd driven David away." A thought occurs to her and her face shatters, sobs spilling forth. "Oh my God, did he die in a car accident from the bad weather? Did I actually chase him to his death that night?"

"No, Mom! Get that thought out of your head. The detective told me he was found alone, no car accident. It looked like he was robbed and hit on the head. They were speculating it could have been a carjacking." I wrap my arms around the woman I've held myself emotionally distant from for over a decade and give myself over to the play of emotions swirling inside me.

Tears trickle down my cheeks as she hugs me. Her voice sounds close to my ear, disbelief coloring the whispered tone. "All these years, and I didn't drive him away."

The simple statement clicks everything into place for me. She felt so awful about what she perceived to be her part in his leaving, that she turned the guilt into anger. Anger at a dead man she thought didn't love her enough to come back and fight through the hard times for her and their children.

Would I have reacted any differently? Would the presumed betrayal have crushed any spark of love inside me, too?

I run a hand down her back. "Let it all go, Mom. Don't let any more anger ruin the rest of your life."

My mother sobs in my arms, the shudders wracking her body as she finally allows her body to grieve for what was and what could have been. Pretty soon I'm crying with her and we're apologizing for all the times we've pushed each other away.

After a while we wash up in separate bathrooms and meet back in the kitchen. I tell her the detective will be here soon and he has some questions for her.

She asks me to stay, saying she'd rather not face him alone. I nod while my heart swells. I never would've expected my father's death to bring us closer, to bridge the gap we've slowly allowed to expand over the years—but strangely enough, it has.

Chapter Twenty

Andrew

"Thanks for filling me in on your call with the doctor. We've always known Mom was a fighter. Maybe her time isn't as close as they think." I pinch the bridge of my nose, worry for my mom and Carla causing a slow headache to build.

"I'm so torn—and feeling guilty as hell because of it," my sister says. "I don't want her to suffer needlessly, but I'm not ready for her to go, either."

"The doctor said they're doing everything they can to make her comfortable, so either way it's out of our hands."

A heavy sigh reaches me and I picture my sibling throwing herself on her couch while we talk. "I know. Doesn't make me feel any less guilty."

"Think about what Carla's family is going through. I'd rather we know what's going on than left hanging for years like they were."

"God, you're right. That would be so much worse."

My phone beeps, indicating another call is coming through. A glance at the screen has me hustling my sister off the line. "Hey, Carla is calling. I'll catch up with you later."

We say a quick goodbye and I click over to Carla. "How are you holding up?"

"Not bad." Her voice sounds rough from old tears.

"Are you on the road home yet? The storm has petered out."

"It's still coming down pretty hard here. I'm going to spend the night. Make sure my mom is okay."

I nod, realize she can't see me and say, "That's a good idea. Have either of you told your sister yet?"

"No. I called and asked her to come over in the morning so we could chat. Just told her it was family business when she badgered me for more info."

"Smart. How did things go with the detective?"

"Okay, I guess. It's all kind of a blur really. He was polite and didn't push when my mom cried. I think he was ruling her out as a suspect as well as digging for any possible leads."

"Do you think their conclusion is right, a carjacking?"

Her breath expels in a whoosh and her exhaustion comes over the line clearly. "I don't know. And honestly, after fifteen years, does it matter? He's gone and he never intended to leave. That's the only detail that's important to us."

We wrap up our call and I settle on the couch, nursing a beer. In about thirty minutes there's a knock at my door. It's Rocko, holding up a six-pack.

"Want to watch the game?"

I let him in. "Beats sitting here stewing."

"Uh-oh. That doesn't sound good."

I shrug and flop back on the couch.

He cracks open a beer and eases down into an armchair nearby. "How'd your date last night go?"

As we watch the game together I proceed to fill him in on all that's happened. I don't go into details about our night together after the restaurant, but the news of Carla's missing father dominates our speculation most of the evening. Her family history explains so much about why she initially acted the way she did with me, hell, with all guys. I'm glad her family has the closure it needs to thrive.

It's been over a week since the detective knocked on Carla's door and changed her family's life forever. The three women agreed not to do a memorial service, as his parents passed away a few years ago and all the couple's mutual friends fell to the wayside little by little over time.

I've seen Carla almost every night, even if I don't stay over. One evening we went to the movies, on Saturday afternoon I helped her at *Dress for Success* again, and Sunday we went to the Bronx Zoo.

That's where I learned she has a deep-seated interest in bears. I bought her a stuffed black bear from the zoo's gift shop, despite her protests that a grown woman doesn't need a fluffy toy animal. Every night I've stayed at her house she's had that cute little bear snuggled under one arm while she sleeps. I've resisted teasing her simply because it's so sweet—like she's allowing herself to relax in a relationship and be herself for the first time.

Each day with her is like an adventure where I learn something new about the transforming woman. She's always been strong, sexy, and confident enough for ten women, but when it's just the two of us, I get to see she has a softer side, too.

A side that's fun to explore, whether with a blindfold, a silk tie, or a can of whip cream. She flips all my buttons without even trying. My prickly fruit has certainly turned into a delicacy to be savored.

As I sit here at my desk, my crackberry burns with another suggestive snippet from my co-worker.

Do you think your piano would hold my weight if we had fun on it?

She's giving me a boner under my desk and driving me wild with distraction.

Maybe, I type back. *As long as we didn't make it a marathon session.*

Ping!

Well, that's really up to you isn't it? ;-)

I unleashed a sexual monster lurking behind her soft blue eyes, and I couldn't be happier. When I suggested last Friday that we tell HR about us dating, she agreed. Turns out those memos and such sent around were intended to discourage interoffice romances, but when it comes right down to it, they don't want to lose two good employees over something happening after hours.

We had to sign disclosures that released the firm from liability, and of course, neither one of us admitted to the *during* work hours naughtiness we had participated in. It's a tentative start in the right direction, which is big for Carla.

A low chime pulls my eyes to the glowing screen lying near my coffee cup.

Have you noticed Barry's biceps?

What the—? Did she mean for that one to come to me? *Should I be noticing his biceps?*

She types back quickly, *I was just thinking of him pinning me down on the conference table and doing me hard. The arms made a nice visual.*

A slow burn begins in my gut. Does she think we're in an open relationship and she can be with other guys in the office? Seeing her with some jerk I have to face day after day would drive me insane.

Not funny, Carla.

Oh? It's okay for you to experiment and tease me beyond all sense of self, but not for me to experiment on another man?

Before I can think of a calm, non-sociopathic rejoinder that will not send her running from me, she calls out over her cubicle partition, "Barry, have you been working out?"

I stand up, a nasty look smeared across my face, to see my lover leaning over her wall batting her eyelashes and smiling sweetly at the accountant across from her.

Poor Barry stumbles in his response. “Er... I ... umm. Yeah, I work out.” I bet he’s never fielded interest from a woman as good-looking as Carla.

The slow burn works its way up and I see red. Carla notices my expression and slips down the aisle, scampering away. I can’t believe after our past week together that she’d play with me like this. Slamming my chair into my desk, I stalk after her, determined to confront her and hash it out.

She takes the stairwell and three other co-workers get there before I do. We all head down to the underground parking garage. The three veer to the right while the curvy blonde holding my attention moves left.

I step past a large concrete support and see no indication of which direction she may have headed. A scrape of sound brings me around and I spot her shadowy outline near a wall, in front of a car hood.

“Carla? What kind of crap are you pulling?”

“Jealous, Andy?” She taunts from the darkness.

My anger spills out. “You flirting in front of me? Hell yes, I’m jealous. How else am I supposed to feel?”

"I know what I feel." Her voice sounds like a deadly purr.

"Oh yeah, and what the hell is that?"

"Turned on."

Her response pulls me up short. "Excuse me?"

"The look on your face at my innocent flirting sent my privates all aquiver."

Just like that, the anger releases from me and a heavy sigh eases from my lungs. She's exploring her sexuality and teasing me—this is something I know how to handle.

I step closer, listening to make sure no one else is nearby. "It did, did it?"

"Oh, yeah."

I reach her side, crossing my arms in a feigned expression of anger. The dim light in the garage casts shadows over her sexy expression—sultry lips parted to reveal a tiny tip of pink tongue. She stares straight into my eyes, while cupping her breasts through her blouse, pushing them up to me in an offering. She licks her lips suggestively and my cock hardens. God, she's gorgeous. Carla can rile me with a simple flick of her tongue.

"I think your stunt was mean," I say.

She pouts, and glances down at my tented slacks. "You're no fun, Andy."

"Yes, I am." I grab her and bend her over the car. "Now, let's see if you're happy with what you stirred up." A gasp escapes her, but she wiggles her ass against the front of my pants, proving she's game. I haul her to a semi-standing position by her short hair, careful to be firm but not cause pain. "Don't make a sound," I whisper, "unless you want everyone in the parking lot to see me fucking you on the hood of this car."

"Damn, Andy," her voice comes out soft and breathy. "I'm so excited right now."

Still holding her hair in one hand, I use my hold to tilt her face up and grab her breast, squeezing it hard. "Pull up your skirt." The rustle of fabric sounds sensual in the cool, dark garage. "Now lower your panties to your knees."

I shift my grip for her to comply, leaving her breast for the few seconds it takes me to free my erection to the cool air. "Are you ready for me?"

A small whimper is all I get in answer, but she reaches between her legs to guide my length in. Warm, moist heat encases me as I slam forward with enough force to bend her back over the car again. My own need to claim this fiery woman and brand her as mine drives me into a red haze of lust.

I let go of her hair, reaching around to her mound. The hard nub of flesh feels like a glowing ember against my hand, betraying her more than aroused state. A low moan seeps into the dimness surrounding us.

"Shh," I whisper in her ear. "You lock those sounds inside or I'll have to put my hand over your mouth like I did in the bathroom."

A spasm courses through her frame at the reminder. She nods her head and clamps her lips shut, the only noise now is our harsh breathing in the deserted garage. Carla spreads two palms on the hood to hold herself steady while I pummel her from behind.

My own need becomes a white-hot center in my middle, clouding everything else. "You're mine, Carla." I say in a low tone that won't carry. "No more flirting with co-workers." I punctuate the last sentence with a rapid pistoning of my hips.

Her inner muscles clench along my length as I rub her mound harder, faster. I knead one breast roughly in my hand, my earlier anger and desperation pouring into our coupling.

"Just you and me for a little while, baby. No one else, you hear?" Letting go of her breast, I hesitate in my actions. I need a response. I need to know she'll give us a decent shot, not run when things get tough. Still rubbing her clit, I lean away to put room between us. Pulling my arm back, I deliver a stinging slap to her left ass cheek. "You hear me, baby? I need an answer."

Carla's body shakes with her need. She nods vigorously, choking out, "Only you." Her response snaps my remaining control. I bow over her back, pumping into her tight little body as hard as I can, wrapping an arm around her middle and holding her close.

Need overwhelms me as I plow to the finish line, fucking her as if my last dying breath was being ripped from my body. Sensations swell through me as I clamp my own mouth down hard on the moans aching to spill forth. Carla's release coats my shaft as her inner walls spasm around me.

My orgasm jets in pulses, spilling out of me in an electrical current of feeling. I'm rattled to the core with the powerful emotions swirling between us. This woman has captured my heart with her passion and I'm not even sure if she's aware of it.

Trailing my hand down her stomach, I hug her to me while remaining locked deep inside.

"God, Andy," her voice comes out in a husky wisp of sound, "that was more than I hoped for when I set out to drive you crazy today."

I smile against her back and rub my cheek over her spine. "You did this on purpose? All those texts and the flirting?"

"Oh, yes," she says on a sigh. "I wanted to see if I could make you lose control again, like after our dinner date. It was sexy as all hell."

I give her one last squeeze before pulling away. "Glad to see you got the reaction you were trying for."

She turns to face me, cupping my cheeks. "I've got way more than I was trying for." Carla leans in and gives me a tender kiss, trailing it out and sending a zing through my blood.

The rest of the workday is uneventful and both of us are able to focus on our jobs. I'm not sure if Carla wants me to come by tonight. I think she's in the mindset now of feeling she needs to set the pace on our new relationship. So, I head home after work, hoping I may hear from her, but not counting on it.

Throwing in some laundry and loading the dishwasher is about all I need to do in my apartment. And the tasks are finished quickly. The weekly maid service takes care of the rest. Grabbing a beer from the fridge, I settle at the piano and start to play. As the notes drift into a song the melody wraps around me, cocooning me in its beauty. My mind is always clearest when I sit behind these keys.

How do I play the rest of this out? I've made my thoughts clear to Carla on other guys. Could she try and push me to my limit to see how I'll react? I like the fun aspects of light domination, but I'm not so sure if I can handle her doing something to deliberately provoke me so I will spank her. That speaks of rage and I don't think I want to combine that with our lovemaking. Although, the little bit of jealousy I felt today certainly made for some hot action in the parking garage.

The whole discipline and contrived *need* to punish someone has never turned me on. My cock twitches in my jeans as I recall how her ass jiggled when I smacked it. But damn, I certainly like playing at the edges of discipline. With the amount of orgasms I've had this week, I can't believe I'm getting a woody just thinking about Carla's bare little bottom.

That time in the storage room...the way she tilted her rump, eager for the next searing smack of my hand or thrust of my fingers deep into her... God, at this rate I'm going to have to take a cold shower or spank off in some tissues.

The doorbell rings and I jerk out of the song, the imagery of my lover's pink cheeks still burned in my mind. Peering through the peephole I see it's Carla, but she's done something different with her hair. I swing the door open and my jaw drops. Carla's wearing a short plaid skirt, white knee socks with saddle shoes, a white blouse and her short hair is pushed back with a headband.

A wicked grin spreads across her face as she pushes past me into my apartment. She glances down at my crotch and smiles. "Don't just stand there with a hard on. Come over here and give me a good spanking."

It sounds like she enjoyed the fun aspects of it, too, and this is her way of asking for more. Always eager to please, I close the door and turn to my exciting new lover. "You like the sting of my palm across your bottom?"

She trembles and bends over the armchair, pushing her ass out on display while lifting her skirt to reveal crisp white cotton panties. Preferring a more intimate approach, I sit on the couch and grab her hips to pull her over my lap. "How about I turn that cute butt pink and then rub the sting away?"

She smiles and turns to face the couch cushions. As my hand flies down to deliver the first smack of the night, the realization that I love this spirited woman shakes me to my very depths.

Chapter Twenty-one

Carla

"Wow, Carla. It sounds like Andy is the right guy for you." Heather takes a sip from her favorite vanilla cappuccino. She smiles—true happiness for me shining from every pore—looking even more adorable with her coffee-foam mustache.

I make a motion she should wipe her lip and she reaches for a napkin. "Is this the part where I say you were right?" I smile to lessen the sting. "Or are you going to wait and spring me with an 'I told you so' when you meet him?"

She waves a hand at me, dismissing the thought. "I don't want, or need, to do that to a friend. All I ever wanted was for you to be happy."

"I am." I can feel the smile stretching across my face. "And you *were* right. I just wasn't ready to see it."

"Isn't that the way it is for most of us? In the end, we all get there when the time is right. Now, about meeting Andy—are we still on for Saturday at the piano bar?"

"Yup. He's taking on a gig every weekend now." I shrug, and look out the window. I'm pleased that I helped encourage him to make the decision, but unsure if saying so will sound like I'm trying to take credit.

"Great! Tony's been looking forward to meeting the man who 'tamed' you."

I choke on my own spit as my indignation barrels to get out. "What the hell?" I cough, clearing my throat. "Like I was a shrew in need of taming?"

Heather laughs, the sound drawing several appreciative glances from nearby male patrons. "Not at all, Carla! He likes you. 'Shrew' never passed his lips. I swear. He knows you encouraged me to dress up when we went dancing and that it was you who pushed me out of my comfort zone the night I met him. If it wasn't for you, I'd never have experienced the wilder side of life." She smiles again, the smile of a sexually confident woman. "And damn, that would have been a crying shame."

The past month has been like a walking dream. While Andy and I manage to hold back during work hours, we've been passionate afterward beyond anything I've ever experienced. A look from his dark blue eyes, the tip of his tongue darting out to moisten his lips, his supple fingers twirling a pen during a meeting... I've got it bad.

I'm not sure when he slipped under my radar and became more, but I can't ignore it anymore. My old fears stemming from childhood when we thought my father left, my mother struggling to provide for my sister and me, no longer haunt me as much. I want Andy, but I don't *need* him.

The realization my mother raised a strong woman who can provide for herself hits me for the first time. It's freeing to not need a man to survive, but to *want* him with every fiber of your being. To have your soul call out when he slides into you... I've never felt anything like it and I don't want to let it go.

Tonight, I plan to tell Andy how I feel. And I'm going to give him a little gift he's sure to love. The furry handcuffs brought a smile to my face when I found them online and pictured us using them.

A knock on the door sends my pulse racing. Glancing down, I quickly adjust my breasts in the red corset to showcase them. I totter over to let Andy in, taking small steps in the fluff-tipped four-inch mules.

Without caring if my neighbors happen to be walking by, I open the door with a dramatic flourish and strike a seductive pose. Andy's eyes bug out for a moment. He's speechless. Motioning him in with a tilt of my head, I shut the door before my boldness exposes me to passerby.

"Well, I guess you didn't really want to watch the movie, did you?" His voice comes out low with an edge to it and before I can respond his hands are all over me, gripping my ass, and tilting me back for a deep kiss.

His instant arousal prods my middle as a thrill of excitement sings through my blood. This man never ceases to draw an immediate reaction from me and I love it.

Andy's lips lock onto mine and he kisses me until my lips swell from the attention. "You look fantastic." He wiggles his eyebrows playfully. "Is this all for me or is another lover crawling out the bathroom window right now?"

I smile at his teasing. "No other lovers needed. You fit the bill quite nicely."

He sighs and runs a warm palm down the back of my thigh, lifting me to cradle his erection against my mound.

"With you dressed like this we'll never get through dinner."

"Where's your control, Mister Super Accountant?"

He chuckles and zeros in on my neck, knowing exactly what his heated kisses do to my insides. "You push even my limits, Carla. This poor number cruncher is only human."

I squirm out of his embrace and saunter into the kitchen, working my ass like a trained stripper. "I ordered Chinese. It arrived before you got here." I turn and laugh at his astonished expression. "Don't worry, I had a robe on when I answered the door, silly."

"Poor delivery guy would think he'd walked into a Penthouse story seeing you answer the door like that." He follows me and gets all grabby hands again until I swat him with a spoon.

"You need to eat. I have plans for us."

"Fine," he grumbles, "can't blame a guy for trying. Especially when you look like you stepped out of a high-end lingerie catalog."

I smile at his appreciation of my efforts, feeling an inner glow at his high praise. I know I'm not cover-model worthy by any stretch of the imagination, but damn, when he stares at me like that I sure as hell feel like I am.

Once Andy wolfed down his food as fast as humanly possible, he stares at me with a burning gaze. I know I can't put him off anymore, nor do I want to. Teasing him with sly glances while we ate got me hot and bothered, too. "I have something for you. Well, two somethings, actually."

"Hmm...? You mean besides the lingerie?"

I rise from my seat at the table and move to the counter, reaching high in a cabinet for two small wrapped boxes. "For you," I say, presenting him with the gifts.

Andy's face softens at the sight of the boxes and a tender look lights his eyes. "Aww, you didn't have to get me anything. And I feel like a shit heel because I don't have a gift in return."

"Oh, come on. Don't be like that. Just open it and enjoy."

He rips off the top of the smallest package first and takes out a small key chain with two keys on it. "What are these to?"

"The first one is for my apartment." Andy's smile grows as I continue, "I want you to come and go as you please. And the second one is for what's in the next box."

He leaves his seat and wraps his arms around me. A kiss burns between us for several moments until he eases back to whisper, "I'll do my best to never disappoint you and keep you happy."

"I know you will, Andy. It was me who needed to come around. And I have. I was so afraid of being left by a man I never wanted to let anyone in, never allowed myself to become intimate. But you showed me being involved with someone doesn't have to be scary and leave me feeling weak."

Looking unsure of what to say, he kisses me again and mumbles a heartfelt, emotional "thank you."

I slide the next package across the counter to him and his face lights up. He rips open the second one to reveal the fuzzy handcuffs. Heat floods his face and the look in his eye becomes wild. "God, woman. What you do to me."

I smile while slipping the cuffs out of the tissue paper. "You mean 'what I plan' on doing to you." Pushing him back to his seat, I nudge him down and press his arms behind the ladder-back chair. I straddle his lap and reach behind to cuff his wrists together, keeping him firmly held in place.

"Holy crap, and I thought the apartment key was big." He lurches up with his hips, brushing his arousal against my center. "I think my dick is ready to explode from both gifts."

I nibble on his ear, eager to send him into a maddened state of arousal—like he does to me. "You better settle down, mister." I firm my tone and try for my sternest police-officer voice. "I've got you dead to rights."

"Yes, sir... er, ma'am." He stutters in his excitement. "Whatever you say. You're the one holding the key."

"Damn straight, I am," I say, rising from his lap and reaching to undo his pants. Andy lifts his hips a bit to help me remove the jeans.

I straddle his lap again, with my thong still on, and lower myself to brush the head of his cock over my satin-covered flesh. "Oh, that feels nice." Andy nods, his eyes glued to the cleavage hovering in front of his face. "I've got something else that needs your attention." Reaching down, I pull first one and then my other breast free to sit atop the corset. The sturdy, boned material forces them high and straight, pointing the aroused nipples directly at Andy's face. "Do a good job and maybe I'll please you."

Andy leans forward and latches onto my right breast. He sucks it in and bites down, then draws back and laves the hard tip. Nibbling deep into my cleavage he makes his way over to the left one. Tickling the peak with the tip of his tongue he sucks just the dark pink areola in and pulls back, elongating the aroused flesh.

He continues back and forth from one breast to the other, sending sparks of sensation through me with every deep pull and little bite. I press my breasts together while undulating my hips over his swollen arousal.

"This is torture not being able to touch you," he says, his voice rough.

"Really?" I gasp. "I don't feel that way."

He swallows a laugh as I cram my breast back into his mouth. The vibration of his humor sends another tingle down my spine. "I think I want your cock now," I say, rising from his lap.

I mince slowly to the counter. Turning my back to him I stick out my ass and run my hands over my hips, catching the sides of the panties on my way. The skimpy material slides along my smooth legs and I step out and kick them aside.

Andy croaks from his chair. "How do you feel about anal sex, Carla?"

I look back over my shoulder, spread my legs a bit, and lean forward on the counter. "I never tried it." Licking two fingers I reach over one hip and slide my fingers down the crack of my bottom to my waiting wetness.

Andy's eyes are glued to my every move. I've never felt so sexy in my entire life.

"Oh, baby," he says. "This is so not fair. I want to stick my tongue into you and feast all night."

"You mean like this?" I say, thrusting two fingers into myself. A low groan comes from the handcuffed man as I steadily pump in and out. Andy's cock pulses back and forth with his heartbeat, bobbing in the light of my kitchen.

On a whim, I pull out my fingers and use one to tease the rim of my ass. "Is this where you want to play next?"

Andy's hungry gaze locks on my circling digit. When I slide one fingertip past the first ring of muscle he lurches in the chair. "You keep that up and I'm going to shoot without you even touching me."

Eyeing his cock, I voice my fears. "I'm not sure you'd fit in my bottom. It feels awfully tight in here."

"Dear God, woman," his hips jerk up and his neck muscles bulge, "either come back over here and mount me or stop talking. The thought of how tight your little virgin ass must be is sending me into a fit."

Deciding he's had more than enough teasing for the night, I do exactly as planned and return to his handcuffed form on the chair. I straddle him again, but this time face away, toward the counter. Sliding down, I guide his cock into my body and start to move.

A low moan fills the air as I settle his erection in deep. "Holy Christ, your pussy feels hot."

I smile while sliding up; savoring every delicious second I've got him under my power. One finger slips between my folds and I tickle the aroused flesh peeking out. I continue the movements, steadily going faster as I bob on his lap. My thighs tense under the driving rhythm I set, threatening to buckle under me.

Ignoring the strain in my legs, and focusing on the hard cock sliding in and out of me, I revel in the moment. To think, I thought I had to issue orders to get what I wanted in bed, when all I really needed was a damn good lover who fired me up.

"Work that clit, sweetheart. I want to feel you writhe when I come."

The creaking of the chair and our rough breathing only adds to the aching desire building in me.

"You've got to have the most gorgeous ass I've ever seen," Andy says in a rush of air. "Once you take these cuffs off me I'm going to spread you on the bed and tongue that tight little hole all night."

Picturing him doing just that, like he did that day weeks ago on the conference table, sends me plummeting over the abyss. A long jagged scream pours from me as I convulse around him. Andy thrusts up, only inches off the chair, forcing himself deeper into me as his own release hits.

My shaky legs finally give and I sink onto his lap, the last pulsations of my orgasm echoing through my whole body. Andy rocks a few more times, coating me deep inside with his pleasure.

Once my breathing stills, I grab some tissues from the table and clean us both up. The shiny key ring glints in the room as I reach behind the chair to uncuff the sexiest man I've ever met.

Andy works his shoulders a few times and leans heavily on the table to get to his feet. "Holy crap. That was freakin' mind blowing." He turns and takes me in his arms, resting some of his weight against me. "How did I ever get so lucky as to have you in my life?"

"Funny, I was thinking the same thing."

"Really?"

"Yes."

He leans in and kisses me, sweat moistening his forehead from our exertions. The emotion I can no longer deny spills into our joining, binding him to me in a way I never knew possible.

The time has come to tell him. I've known him for months even if I only saw the real Andy more recently. The words burn inside, eager to leap into the air between us. I reach up, placing my hands on his cheeks, and ease his lips away from mine.

Staring deep into his eyes, I utter the three words I haven't said to a man since my father died. "I love you."

His eyes widen and I swear I see a glint of moisture in them. "I love you, too." His arms crush me to his chest in a fierce hug. "And if I have my way, I'll be saying that to you every day for the rest of our lives."

My own vision blurs as I press my lips to his, feeling the happiest I've ever been in my entire existence.

~~*~~

About the Author: C.J. Ellisson lives in northern Virginia with her husband, two children, two dogs, and a fluffy black cat who makes her sneeze. Unlike most full-time authors, she's also battling severe chronic illness. C.J. works daily to put her Lupus into remission and continues to fight numerous bacterial infections while her immune system slowly attacks her body. She turned to writing when she could no longer work outside the home and claims the escape of penning contemporary erotic romance, urban fantasy, and erotica. has helped save her sanity

*Avoiding Mr. Righ*t is the second book in the *Walk on the Wild Side* series and there are currently five novels and at least two novellas planned, with more to be added if there is enough reader interest.

Books in the *Wild Side* series :

Heather & Tony books: ***Vanilla on Top ~ Vanilla Twist* (due out Jan 2014) ~ *Vanilla Spice* (due out 2014)**
Spin off couples: ***Avoiding Mr. Right ~ Loving Ms. Wrong* (due out March 2014)**

Join C.J. Ellisson's Monthly Newsletter to Receive Notice of:

~ Contests
~ Free Reads & Sneak Peeks
~ Book Signings & Appearances
~ Online Reader Events
~ Upcoming Sales
~ New Releases

To sign up, copy this site address into your browser's address bar: **bit.ly/cj-news**

MORE places to connect with C.J.:

Website: cjellisson.com
Facebook: facebook.com/C.J.EllissonFanPage
Online Book Club: facebook.com/groups/urbanfantasybc
Street Team: facebook.com/groups/cjeseethe

Do you miss signed books? C.J. offers free, full-color signed 4x6 postcards of all her novels to readers who've left honest reviews on any retailer or book reviewing website. To obtain yours, please email your review URLs to admin@cjellisson.com with your mailing address--international readers welcome!

Acknowledgements

My readers greatly influence my career and the choices I make in business. I listen to them and weigh their opinions when deciding on the next project to tackle, cover to select, or reader convention to attend. I'm grateful they reach out to me on Facebook and have become my friends. Some authors may prefer to be reclusive, but I'm not one of them. Thank you for being part of this incredible journey with me.

A big thanks goes to my editor, Tina Winograd. We met years ago on writing.com and I can honestly say you're the best thing that's happened to my work in a long time. Thank you for standing by me no matter what and for being a friend.

I've met quite a few incredible authors this past year. Whether through social networking, in person, or via email, they have buoyed up my confidence and helped me to see what an amazing community of peers I have. Thank you for sharing your wisdom and for supporting me. I get a secret thrill whenever I hear a fellow writer has enjoyed my work. Our time is so limited (and our TBR piles so tall) I'm honored they would spend their precious resource on something I created.

As always, thank you, Peter. The past few months have brought a lot of change in our lives and you never cease to amaze me with your unwavering support and belief in my career.

~~*~~

www.ingramcontent.com/pod-product-compliance
Lightning Source LLC
Chambersburg PA
CBHW051949220626
47052CB00004B/864
* 9 7 8 1 9 3 8 6 0 1 1 8 7 *